Mexican Shoot-Out

TOM PARRY

A Black Horse Western

ROBERT HALE · LONDON

© Tom Parry 2004
First published in Great Britain 2004

ISBN 0 7090 7581 2

Robert Hale Limited
Clerkenwell House
Clerkenwell Green
London EC1R 0HT

Typeset by
Derek Doyle & Associates, Liverpool.
Printed and bound in Great Britain by
Antony Rowe Limited, Wiltshire

Mexican Shoot-Out

Sergeant Callaghan of the Eleventh Cavalry travels over the border to Mexico on a mission which he assumes will be uneventful. But things start to go wrong when he and his companion, the beautiful Maria Lopez, almost die of exhaustion in the desert and seem destined to become the victims of a band of Apaches.

Callaghan continues to defy death when the mayor of San Caldiz plans to kill him to level an old score. Further trouble is on the way when a consignment of money to start a bank in the town attracts the attention of a gang of outlaws. Soon Callaghan is in the middle of a shoot-out between the warring parties. As if that were not danger enough, Apaches appear on the scene. Can Callaghan survive bullet and arrow?

CHAPTER 1

Sergeant Paul Callaghan stood stiffly to attention. His eyes were firmly fixed on the face of his superior officer who was sitting at his desk in front of him. On the rare occasions when he had been summoned to the office of Major Linton it had usually been because he was in some sort of trouble or other. He had no idea what was the reason behind his present appearance in front of his superior officer, but he would guess that the news was not going to be good.

Major Linton's stern face added weight to Paul's intuition. The major had a lined face which together with his white hair and white moustache signified that he had been in the US Eleventh Cavalry for a considerable number of years. Just how many years there had been were emphasized by the major's first statement.

'I've been in the cavalry for more years than I

care to remember, Callaghan, and just occasionally I do something which is against my better judgement.'

Paul correctly deduced that this opening gambit was the kind which didn't require a reply. He wisely said nothing.

'I have come to the conclusion that this is one of those occasions.' The major picked up a sheet of paper which lay on his desk. 'Do you know what this is?'

'No, sir,' replied Paul.

'It is a summary of your progress so far in the Eleventh Cavalry. Although come to think of it, perhaps progress is too strong a word. Progress implies that you would normally be going forward. Well, looking at this report, you seem determined to go backwards. Without checking the reports of the rest of the members of the regiment I am reasonably positive that you are the only one who, in five years, progressed from a private to a corporal, then to a sergeant, and eventually to a captain. And then went back down to a sergeant again. What are you trying to do, Callaghan? Is it your aim to go back down to corporal and then back down to private again?'

Paul decided that this again was another of the major's rhetorical questions. He said nothing.

'As I said this is against my better judgement.' The major glanced at the report as if to confirm something. 'It says here that you speak Spanish.'

Paul spoke for only the second time since entering the office.

'That's right. My family moved over the border to keep a farm near San Caldiz when I was nine years old. I went to school in the town for several years. Then we settled back in Texas.'

'That's one of the reasons why I'm sending you to Mexico. Your knowledge of Spanish could come in useful.'

So he was going to be sent to Mexico. Well at least that would be a change. He was sick and tired of going out on patrols searching for Apaches. The Indians would have stolen a horse or two from one of the dozens of small farms which were dotted around the place. The major would send out a patrol as a matter of course. The Apaches would have disappeared over the border. Although the cavalry were not supposed to venture into Mexico they would tacitly ignore the instructions and follow the Indians for a few miles into Mexico. Not that it made any difference. They would invariably return empty-handed, the Apaches in the meantime having sold the horses to some Mexicans who were always eager to buy cheap horses.

'Have you been back to San Caldiz recently?'

'No, sir. Not since the family left the town.'

'Well, you'll be going there on this mission. I can't emphasize how important this is. If the result is satisfactory I might even consider reinstating you to the rank of captain. Although I'm not definitely promising you anything.'

When would the old fool come to the point? What was this task which he was about to be entrusted with?

'In the first place,' continued the major. 'I have some important dispatches which I want you to deliver to the Mayor of San Caldiz. His name is Señor Raoul del Mancho. If you haven't been to San Caldiz for several years I don't expect you have heard of him.'

Paul kept a straight face. The last thing he wanted would be to let the major know that he was aware of Señor Raoul and his political activities. So that was why he was being sent to San Caldiz, to deliver some dispatches to Raoul. Well that didn't seem like a difficult task. If anything it would be a nice relaxing holiday. He should even be able to spend a few days in the cantinas in San Caldiz. Yes, he was already looking forward to the mission.

'There is one other thing.' For the first time since Paul had entered the office, the major paused and appeared slightly uncomfortable.

'Yes, sir?'

'You will be taking a companion with you.'

Paul's hopes of having a busman's holiday began to sink on hearing the words. Instead of having a few days on his own which would allow him the freedom to spend some of that time in the relaxing atmosphere of some of the cantinas he was going to be a nursemaid to some young trooper or other.

'As I said if you make a success of this mission you could be promoted back to your rank of captain. On the other hand if you make a mess of it, I will personally see that you will be demoted to the rank of private. Moreover you will stay at that rank for as long as you are in the cavalry. Do I make myself clear?' The major snapped the words out in his best parade-ground manner.

'Yes, sir.'

'Right. Your companion will be a woman. Her name is Maria Lopez. She is going to San Caldiz to marry the mayor.'

Paul, who had already began to have doubts about the mission, now realized that those doubts had been considerably magnified.

CHAPTER 2

Paul found himself involuntarily glancing across at his companion. They had been riding together for half an hour and he found that the outstanding beauty of Maria Lopez was still fascinating him. Whether she was aware of his glances was not obvious from her demeanour. She rode her grey mare with a perfect posture. Indeed Paul could not find anything about her which was less than perfect.

When he had been introduced to her by the major the previous evening he had been expecting to meet a typical Mexican woman. From his experience they tended to be rather shorter than American women. Another difference was that while many American women were rather skinny, Mexicans were plumper. But it was obvious that Maria Lopez was not a typical Mexican. When the major had introduced them Paul's look of admiration at meeting such a stunning beauty was not lost on his superior officer, who smiled to himself at Paul's reaction.

The major had enlightened Paul later that Maria was part Aztec, part Spaniard. This accounted for her classical profile with her high forehead, aquiline nose and full lips. Her jet-black hair was pinned on top of her head and this emphasized the slender curve of her neck. She had green eyes which had stared unflinchingly at Paul when they were introduced.

'Pleased to meet you,' she said, offering her gloved hand.

'Maria has been in Europe for several years,' supplied the major. 'At an expensive finishing-school,' he added.

They had started off at the crack of dawn. Paul had explained that by starting early they should be across the desert before the sun reached its high point.

'I see,' she had replied.

Paul had been half-expecting her to be late for the start of their journey, but he was pleased to see that she was arriving at the stables at the same time as himself. He arranged for their water bottles to be filled. These were a vital component in their travelling possessions. If, for some reason they were forced to spend a whole day in the desert then their water bottles could be their sole means of survival.

'It's about twenty miles across the desert,' Paul explained. 'With luck we should manage to get across before the heat becomes too unbearable.'

'I see,' she replied.

Paul reflected that she seemed to be a girl – no, a woman – of few words. As they rode side by side he amused himself in trying to guess how old she was. Eighteen? Nineteen? Twenty? Of course in Mexico they could get married at fourteen. But he was positive that she was several years older than that. She was wearing a cloak which partly concealed her figure but as she rode it would fly open now and then to reveal a glimpse of the form of a mature woman.

Several of his companions in the sergeant's mess had expressed their jealousy the previous night when it had been disclosed that he would be accompanying Maria to San Caldiz. They had spotted her when she had ridden into the camp on the stage. Female visitors to the camp were rare and one as beautiful as Maria was as unusual as snow in summer. Paul had to field the ribald comments he received from the other sergeants during their meal-time.

'You lucky dog, a few days in San Caldiz, accompanied by the beautiful Maria. How did you come to be chosen?'

'Because I'm the only handsome one here among you ugly lot.'

'Try to spend a night in the desert. It gets so cold that she will have to cling to you to keep warm.'

He had explained that she was getting married to someone else.

'That hasn't stopped you in the past,' voiced one of the sergeants. 'I remember how at Lambert's wedding you disappeared with the bride behind the stables for about ten minutes.'

'I only did it to win a bet,' countered Paul. 'You lot bet me that I couldn't entice her away from the wedding-party for ten minutes. Come to think of it a few of you still owe me five dollars for winning that bet.'

The sergeants hastily changed the subject.

'I hear she's come from Europe. From Paris,' announced one.

'You know what they say about French women,' declared another.

'They say they're all hot stuff,' chimed in another, to raucous laughter.

'She's not French, she's half Spaniard,' said Paul, as he stood up and left the table.

'What's the other half?' demanded another.

'Aztec,' replied Paul.

'They used to believe in human sacrifices,' professed another. 'If I were you I'd watch my step. I wouldn't leave any knives around after you've had a meal.'

The laughter echoed behind Paul as he left the

mess in order to go to the stables and check the horses.

Now the conversation sifted through his mind as they rode at a steady gallop. He pushed the horse as hard as he dared so they could cover as much ground as possible before the heat from the sun began to hit them. They had already been riding for an hour and from time to time Paul's gaze shifted to the red ball in the sky which was soon going to begin to torment them. He had travelled through the desert often enough to know that the first stage of discomfort was going to be the sweat on the brows. This would gradually increase until a little would drop into the eyes. This would sting sharply and for a brief moment it would blur your vision. You would wipe it away and wait for the next moment of discomfort to arrive. This would be the beginning of a couple of hours which would feel like a personal battle between yourself and the maddening red ball in the sky.

At some stage you would stop. Although your tongue would be caked and feel like baked leather your first priority would be to give the horse its water from the water bottle attached to your saddle. Only when your horse had satisfied its thirst would you be allowed to drink. This was one of the regulations which had been drummed into him during his time in the cavalry. Always look after your horse first. Of the many rules which had been instilled into him it was the one which made the most sense.

Another piece of essential advice which had been drummed into him by the first sergeant who had shouted at him on the parade ground was: 'Always watch out for rattlers'. It had became second nature for him to follow that advice. But he realized with instant horror that the advice hadn't been instilled into a certain female who had spent her formative years in Paris. Her horse reared as the rattler struck. Two sounds rent the air simultaneously – the almost human scream of pain of the horse. The second was definitely a human cry – it was Maria's cry of shock and horror.

A third sound came almost immediately afterwards – it was sound of a revolver being fired as Paul shot the rattler's head off. Maria in the meantime was struggling to not be squashed under the horse which had fallen to its knees and was beginning to roll over. She managed to release herself from the stirrups in time. She jumped to one side as the animal rolled on to its back.

It presented a pathetic sight. Its eyes seemed to be beseeching Paul to help it out of its agony.

Maria's voice cut across his thoughts.

'For God's sake put her out of her agony.'

Paul stepped towards the mare. He put his revolver to her head and pulled the trigger.

Five minutes later they were on their way again.

This time Maria was riding behind Paul. In addition to the extra weight of the new passenger Paul's horse was carrying a couple of water bottles which Paul had untied from the dead horse. Paul knew that the first part of the journey had witnessed a tragic accident. But the second part could be equally eventful in terms of distress since the remorseless sun was now beating down on the two people who were forced to travel slowly through the desert.

CHAPTER 3

They had been riding for about half an hour. Paul's horse which had started off gamely at a slow trot was now reduced to a slow walking pace. It was obvious that each step was agony as the horse toiled in the sweltering heat.

Paul pulled up. Maria jumped off the horse and he followed her by dismounting. He untied the water bottles. He gave one to Maria who accepted it without a word. With the other he began to quench the horse's insatiable thirst.

He was concentrating on the horse and so didn't notice how much water Maria had drunk. When he did give her his full attention he was shocked to find that she had almost emptied the water bottle he had given her.

'We're still just only over half-way,' he said. 'There are only two full water bottles left. And the horse will want one.'

'I'm sorry. I didn't know.'

Well you should have known, he had almost voiced the angry thought when he suddenly realized that it had been his fault, not hers. He was used to travelling through the desert. They came out here regularly on patrols when they were chasing the Apaches. To conserve water when you were riding in the desert was second nature to him. But all this was new territory to her. She had probably never travelled through even a few miles of desert in her life. And the Diablo Desert, as the Mexicans called it from the days when Texas had been a part of their territory, was definitely one of the largest in the territory.

'Take your cloak off.'

'Wh-at?'

'You'll get more protection from the sun if you take your cloak off and pin it on your head so it will protect the back of your neck.'

She took it off. She arranged it so that it covered her head and hung down her back. When she had finished pinning it up she said:

'Is that all right?'

'Yes, you'll get more protection that way. Right. Let's go.'

They set off again. The horse, having rested for a few minutes and having been watered, started off with a new spring in its step. But Paul knew that this was only a temporary respite and within a mile or so he would again begin to falter.

As they rode along he kept involuntarily glancing at the sun. It would soon be reaching the point high in the sky where its heat would turn the desert into an oven. Any unfortunate traveller in the desert from that point on would be literally baking.

'Can you ride bare-back, Sergeant?'

'Call me Paul.'

'Can you, Paul?'

'Yes, I can.'

'Suppose we throw away the saddle. This will mean that the horse will have less weight to carry.'

He admitted it was a good idea. The saddle weighed several pounds. Without it the horse would be able to struggle on a few miles further before at last it became too much for it to carry two people on its back.

'Right. We'll get rid of the saddle.'

They dismounted. Paul took his rifle from its sheath. He also untied the remaining water bottle.

'I'll carry the bottle,' said Maria.

They set off once again, this time with Paul carrying the rifle and holding on to the reins with his free hand. He could feel Maria's body pressing behind him. The unbidden thought came to him that the sergeants back in the mess would unmercifully barrack him if they found out that he travelled for miles though the desert with the desirable Maria clinging on to him.

For a while the horse seemed to enjoy its new freedom without having the weight of the saddle on its back. It showed its relief by stepping forward more confidently. But in a short while it dropped back to its previous slow movement.

The sun was now focusing mercilessly on the slow-moving humans on the horse. Paul had suffered in the searing heat of the desert before and so was partly prepared for it. Only partly, however, since on previous occasions he had been accompanied by several of his companions. He had always drawn strength from their companion-ship. He had known that if the worst came to the worst they always brought a couple of spare horses with them. How he could do with a spare horse now.

He wondered how Maria was faring. It was defi-nitely harder travelling without having a saddle under them. They had been travelling for about half an hour without any communication between them after they had discarded the saddle. Their mode of travel was definitely different from what she had been used to in the sophisticated cities in Europe where she had spent her previous few years. As if in unspoken answer to his question as to how she was faring he felt her slip from behind him. He turned to try to grab her, but he was too late. She slid to the ground. Instinctively Paul jumped down as well.

She presented a dishevelled figure as she lay on the sand. Her skirt had drawn up around her knees and she was revealing a shapely pair of legs. She didn't seem aware of Paul's admiring glance as she groped behind her.

'I saved the water bottle,' she exclaimed, producing it triumphantly.

'The only problem is, we've lost the horse,' stated Paul.

True enough the horse, revelling in its new found freedom, had galloped away. It was now about half a mile ahead of them and obviously intent on increasing the gap even further.

'Oh – *shit!*' she exclaimed in frustration.

'Is that what they taught you in that expensive finishing-school?'

'You'd be surprised what I learnt,' she replied, as she brushed the sand from her clothes.

CHAPTER 4

He was dying for a drink and he guessed that his companion by his side had the same overpowering desire. But he knew that they had to ration the precious water in the bottle. It was their only chance of survival.

They hadn't spoken since they had set off on their trek across the burning desert. True, when they had seen the horse gallop away Maria had asked him whether there was any way of stopping it. His reply that the only way to put a halt to its escape would be to shoot it had effectively ended their brief conversation.

He had half-expected her to ask whether they would make it to the Rio Grande. In which case his reply would have to have been: it's in the lap of the gods. He had been long enough in Fort Manton to have heard stories of people being lost in the desert. And their bones being found some time later, picked clean by the vultures. A few weeks ago they had come across an unidentifiable skull and bones. Out of respect they had buried them where they had been found. At the time he had never guessed that in a short while he could be facing the same prospect of his bones being left lying somewhere out here.

He glanced at his companion. She was walking steadily by his side. Her face was flushed and sweat stood out on her brow. Now and then she wiped it away with the back of her hand. He wished he could say something comforting to her, like: We'll be out of this searing heat in a short while. But he knew it wouldn't be true. If his calculations were correct they still had about six miles to walk. Six miles with the sun at its highest. Six miles of agony with the sun burning down on them.

'Why don't you take off your jacket?'

'What?'

'Why don't you take off your jacket? It will be less weight for you to carry. Then you can turn your shirt-collar up.'

'It's a good idea.'

He took off his jacket. He emptied the few belongings – the tin of ammunition, his penknife, a handkerchief and a photograph into his trouser pockets. She glanced curiously at the motley collection – particularly the photograph. He sensed her curiosity but gave no indication that he had observed her interest.

He used the enforced stop to open the water bottle.

'Two mouthfuls,' he informed her.

She obligingly took a mouthful, then held it in her mouth before swallowing it. She repeated the act.

Paul took his own ration and fixed the top back on the bottle.

They started off again. The sun, which had been beating down mercilessly before, seemed to have gathered a new strength. It was now a personal battle between the glowing orb in the sky and the two people struggling to reach the safety of the river. The sun was saying: I'll get you before you reach your goal.

The only way to try to beat the scorching ball was to concentrate on each step. Try to beat the bloody thing by counting each step. Imagine you are on a parade-ground and the sergeant is barking at you: Pick them up, left, right, left. right. . . .

The trouble was it only helped for a moment. The blistering heat again took over. You could no longer think clearly. There was a red mist in front of your eyes. For a brief moment you even forgot where you were. A picture came unbidden to your mind that you were in hell. They say that hell is a warm place, but surely it isn't as warm as this. You shake your head to try to clear your mind of such thoughts. The only thing that happened was that the mental picture changed to one of a lake of water. Delicious cool water. The picture was so plain that he felt that he only had to put out his hand to reach it. At least that was how it seemed in the first place. But then it seemed to be receding as he went towards it. The lake seemed to be mocking him. Perhaps if he ran he would be able to catch it up. He pulled himself up just in time. Oh, God! He must be getting delirious.

He glanced involuntarily at his companion. She was staring stonily ahead. Rivulets of sweat were running down her face. She looked like an ancient Aztec who was going to be sacrificed at the altar of the sun god. Even in his befuddled state he could recognize the probable truth in the thought. She *was* going to be sacrificed before the sun god. And he with her.

A short while later he called a halt.

'We'll have some water.'

Was that croak his voice? He offered her the bottle. She hesitated before accepting it. Perhaps she had realized it would be her last drink.

She accepted the bottle. She held it up for a few seconds as though proposing a toast. If Paul had been able to smile he would have done so. But his lips were so thick and cracked that he doubted whether he would ever be able to smile again.

She handed him the bottle. He took a grateful

pull, then realized with horror that he had emptied it. He tossed it away in disgust.

'How much further to go?' she asked.

'Not much further,' he lied.

CHAPTER 5

Three Apaches were riding though the desert. They usually kept away from the desert in the heat of the day, preferring to stay close to the Rio Grande. But today, while riding along the edge of the river, they had spotted a horse drinking thirstily from the river.

They approached the horse, which was so preoccupied with quenching its thirst that it was for a moment unaware of the riders. When the animal eventually raised its head it was to be greeted by a coil of rope from a lasso, which effectively banished any ideas it might have harboured of galloping away.

The leader of the Apaches, a warrior named Lion in the Hills examined the horse closely.

'It's a cavalry horse,' he announced.

'How do you know?' demanded one of his companions, a warrior named Eyes like a Hawk.

'By the mark on its thigh,' retorted their leader. 'It's a figure eleven.'

'That means the horse comes from the Eleventh Cavalry,' said the third member of the group, named He Who Always Knows Best.

'The question is what is it doing here?' demanded their leader, stroking its head as though half-expecting to find an answer by doing so.

'Where's its saddle?' demanded Eyes Like a Hawk.

'There's only one way we'll find the answer,' said He Who Always Knows Best.

'What's that?' demanded their leader.

'We'll have to go into the desert to find out. We can easily follow the horse's trail back into the desert.'

'When we find it, we'll be able sell the saddle for about twenty dollars,' said the leader, who felt that he was in danger of losing his position to the upstart know-all.

So they set about retracing the horse's trail through the desert.

'We can't go too far into the desert,' said Eyes Like a Hawk. 'Not in this heat.'

They had ridden about two miles and there was no sign of the horse's saddle, or its previous rider.

'I think this is far enough.' Their leader held up his hand in the accepted manner which he had observed officers of the Eleventh Cavalry adopt to make their underlings comply with their command.

'I think you're right,' said He Who Always Knows Best.

They were about to turn their horses when a shout from their third companion stopped them in their tracks.

'I can see two figures lying in the sand,' he cried, excitedly.

The heat of the sun cast a haze over the sand and their leader could see nothing. However he knew that Eyes Like a Hawk had the sharpest eyes of the three and if he said there were two figures lying in the sand then the chances were that he was right.

'We'll go ahead carefully,' he announced.

They had only been advancing at a walking-pace from the time they had set out from the river, since they had been busy checking the sand in order to follow the trail of the strayed horse. Their steady form of progress didn't change. The only change, in fact, was that they now scanned the terrain ahead instead of looking down at the sand in front of their mounts.

In a short while they were all able to see the figures in the sand.

'It looks like a man and a woman,' said Eyes Like a Hawk.

'Can you see if he's wearing a uniform?' asked the leader.

'No, he's not wearing a uniform,' came the definite reply.

'We'll still go carefully,' said their leader.

They approached the figures who were lying in the sand. Soon the other two were able to confirm that the man wasn't wearing a uniform. Some of their caution dissolved. Here were two figures who were obviously dead. They had suffered the same slow end to their lives as dozens of other travellers through the desert. They had finally run out of water. This would have been followed by their collapsing in the sand. Then unconsciousness would have been a blissful relief. To think that they were only two miles from the river when they collapsed and died.

These thoughts flitted through the mind of Lion in the Hills as he approached the two figures in the sand, having discarded caution. He was jerked back to a sudden change in the picture he had been painting in his mind by the unexpected movement of the man. The movement was followed by another which was so sudden that he was unable to counter it.

'All of you get down from your horses,' said

Paul. The command was emphasized by the unwavering barrel of the rifle which was pointing straight at them.

CHAPTER 6

A quarter of an hour later Paul and Maria reached the Rio Grande. Paul had reclaimed his own horse and Maria was happily riding one of the Apaches' horses. The other two Apache horses had been scared off into the desert by the sounds of Paul's rifle firing aimlessly into the air. It would take their owners a considerable time to retrieve them.

Not only had Paul taken one of the Apaches' horses, he had also relieved them of two of their water bottles. The three Apaches had watched sullenly while Maria and Paul had quenched their thirst. Eventually Paul had demanded:

'How far is it to the river?'

He Who Always Knows Best had held up two fingers.

'Two miles?' asked Paul.

The Apache nodded.

Paul produced a handful of coins. He counted out five dollars. He indicated to Lion in the Hills to step forward and take them. The Apache did so, secretly delighted that the cavalryman had given them to him and not to He Who Always Knows Best.

'These are for the horse,' said Paul. 'Although I expect you stole it in the first place.'

Maria, too, fumbled in her dress and produced a purse. She produced three dollars.

'One for each of you. For saving our lives,' she said simply.

When they reached the Rio Grande they didn't hesitate, they rode the horses straight into the river. They pulled up when the water reached their thighs. Maria reached down and splashed some of the delicious cool water on to her face. Paul followed suit. Who would have thought that the simple action of splashing your face with water could bring such relief?

He glanced at his companion. Having splashed water over her face again and again she had found an even better way of enjoying the coolness of the river. She had jumped from her horse into the river and was now standing up to her waist in the water. She was busily scooping large handfuls of water and splashing it over the top half of her body. As she did so she was whooping happily like a schoolgirl.

After a while she turned her attention to Paul.

'Come on in, you sissy,' she shouted. 'Are you

afraid of getting wet?'

Paul knew that his first duty lay with the horses. But they seemed quite happy to stand in the river under the shelter of the trees and feel its coolness on their flanks. Paul accepted Maria's invitation and jumped into the water.

While Maria was whooping by his side, Paul ducked his head under the water. He held it under for fully a minute before breaking the surface. When he did so he shook his head like a terrier coming out of the river.

Maria smiled at his action. She copied it by ducking her own head into the water. When she came up her hair was plastered to her head and beads of water hung on her face. She looked younger than when they had set out on their memorable ride. At that time Paul had assumed that she was about twenty, but now she looked several years younger.

She smiled happily at him as they stood in the water a few feet apart. Paul inched slowly towards her. The smile stayed on her face. He moved closer until they were almost touching. She was still staring at him intently. What followed seemed to Paul as inevitable as night following day. He kissed her.

It was a long kiss. It held all the pent-up passion of two people who had been alone in the desert and who had thought half an hour ago that their lives would come to an end in that burning heat. It held all the joy of the fact that they were alive. Even though their lips were still aching from the effects of the burning desert neither seemed to want to end the kiss. Paul was aware that the wet body pressing against his was that of a very desirable female. Maria had put her hands on Paul's face to hold him closer, while his arms were entwined around her waist. Their moment of passion however came to an abrupt end when they both heard a shout from the bank.

They broke apart. There were several Mexicans seated on their horses on the opposite bank. Paul guessed there were about ten of them. The one who held his attention, however, was Señor Raoul del Mancho.

His face was like thunder.

'This behaviour is not what I would expect from my future wife,' he shouted.

CHAPTER 7

An hour or so later Paul was seated in a cantina. An almost empty bottle of tequila stood on the table in front of him. He was the only customer in the cantina. Indeed most of the owner's regular customers were doing the sensible thing at this time of the afternoon – they were having a siesta. The owner of the cantina, whose name was Sanchez, should also be having a siesta. But he had been disturbed by a loud banging on his door as if the tax man was demanding entry.

When he had opened the door he had found an American standing there. He had assumed he was an American because he was tall and fair-skinned. The stranger had explained that he wanted a drink. Normally Sanchez would have refused to serve him. But there were two things about the American's request which made him change his mind. In the first place he asked for the drink in perfect Spanish. In Sanchez's experience there were very few Americans who spoke perfect Spanish. The other thing that helped Sanchez decide to open the cantina for him was the expression on his face. It was a sad expression. It was the sort of sadness which the Father would see regularly when people went to the Church of the Blessed Virgin to confess their sins. Sanchez, too, recognized a man who was troubled in his mind. And if the American chose to come to his cantina to help get rid of his troubled thoughts then it was up to Sanchez, as an upright citizen, to help him.

'Another bottle.' The stranger had emptied the bottle of tequila and was holding it up as evidence.

Sanchez obligingly brought another bottle from behind the counter.

'Are you staying in San Caldiz long?' he demanded, as he opened the bottle.

'I'll be going back over the border tomorrow,' Paul informed him.

'So you're not staying for the fiesta?' enquired Sanchez.

Paul shook his head. 'I don't think so.'

'Raoul has declared the day a public holiday. He's getting married in the morning. Afterwards there'll be wine, women and song.' Sanchez rubbed his hands excitedly at the thought. 'I've ordered fifty extra bottles of tequila. They say the bride-to-be is one of the most beautiful women you have ever seen.'

Paul didn't reply. Instead he took a long swig at his drink.

'Raoul is the mayor of the town,' continued Sanchez.

'I know,' Paul informed him.

'I didn't know his fame had spread to America,' said Sanchez, slightly surprised.

'I know Raoul because I used to live here,' Paul said, emptying his glass. Sanchez hastily stepped forward to refill it.

'I wondered how you spoke Spanish so well.'

'I lived in San Caldiz when I was younger. I went to school with Raoul.'

'So you know all about him?'

'I know that he's one of the biggest crooks I've ever met.'

Alarm flitted across Sanchez's face. Although it was obvious there was nobody else in the cantina, Sanchez still looked around to confirm it.

'Don't say such things about Raoul,' he said, dropping his voice to a whisper.

'It's the truth,' said Paul, slurring his words slightly.

'I know it's the truth. And you know it's the truth,' said Sanchez. 'But if you go outside this cantina saying such things you will end up in jail even though you are an American.'

'Raoul was a criminal when we were just school-boys,' continued Paul. 'He's just become a bigger criminal as time passed.'

'So you knew him in school,' said Sanchez. 'What's your name?'

'Paul Callaghan. My father had a farm to the west of the town.' Paul supplied the information and followed it with a long swig of his tequila.

'There were lots of farms there at one time,' replied Sanchez. 'But most of them are deserted now. They've gone to rack and ruin.'

'Ours was a thriving farm.' There was a belligerent note in Paul's voice.

'It's got nothing to do with the farms, the fact that they're deserted,' said Sanchez, hastily. 'It's all down to Luis.'

'Who's Luis?'

'He's the *bandito* who lives up in the mountains. Now and then he and his gang come down and raid the farms. They take away the horses and the livestock. That's why most of the farms are now deserted.'

'Why doesn't Raoul do something about Luis?'

'He would like to. He's already tried on two occasions to fight Luis up in the mountains. But Luis knows the territory. Raoul lost the battle on both occasions. He cannot afford to go up into the mountains and try a third time. If he lost again he would lose so much face that the people would be bound to turn against him. It would be the end of Raoul.'

'Good old Luis,' said Paul, raising his glass in salute.

'You shouldn't say such things,' said a shocked Sanchez.

CHAPTER 8

Paul was awakened the following morning by the din outside his lodgings. It didn't take a genius to work out that the fiesta had began. He had originally intended to get up early and ride away from San Caldiz before the festivities started, but due to the tequila he had drunk last night his resolve to awake early had been dashed. When he looked at his watch he found out that it was already mid-morning.

When he went downstairs the landlady informed him that the fiesta had already started.

'I know,' said Paul, shortly.

'My other guests have gone to see it,' she informed him.

Paul knew that the 'other guests' comprised a retired Army officer, his wife and a shady character who looked like a small-time thief or perhaps a pickpocket.

He accepted the tortillas the landlady had put in front of him.

'The church service will be starting soon in the Church of the Blessed Virgin,' she said. 'I don't want to miss seeing them when they come out of the church.'

It was a broad hint to Paul to hurry up with his breakfast and leave the lodging-house. Paul's response was to eat his breakfast slowly in order to irritate her. When he had finished she had placed his only piece of luggage, his rifle, by his table, as an even broader hint that he was no longer a welcome guest in her house.

She emphasized her displeasure with her next statement.

'We don't like guns in this house.'

'Oh, I don't know,' said Paul, mildly. 'They come in useful sometimes for killing vermin.'

This time she showed her displeasure at the American by sniffing and stating pointedly, 'The mayor has banned all guns during the fiesta.'

Paul didn't bother to reply. He paid her for his night's lodgings and went out into the street. He stood for a moment in the bright sunlight. A small party of revellers passed him. One of the young members of the party turned round and called back to him.

'Come and join us, we're going to Ronaldo's.'

Paul had no idea of the whereabouts of

Ronaldo's. A lot of things had changed since he had lived in San Caldiz.

'No, thanks,' he replied.

He had intended collecting his horse from the stables and riding out of the town. But somehow he found his footsteps, as if by their own volition, taking him the opposite way. It was the direction that led to the Church of the Blessed Virgin.

The crowd outside the church was huge. It seemed as though the whole of the town had gathered there. All available spaces outside the church, including the graveyard were packed with sightseers. Paul managed to squeeze inside the gate. He inched slowly along the wall until he came to a vantage point opposite the church door. Every available space on the wall had been taken up, mainly by children whose parents had deposited them there so that they would be able to get a good view of the bride and groom. Paul selected a couple of youths who were seated on the wall.

'I'll give you fifty pesos each for your seat,' he informed them.

It was an exchange too good to be refused. They were already bored with having to sit and wait for the bride and groom to appear. They accepted the coins with alacrity.

Paul took their place. He was seated about fifty yards from the church door. He would have a perfect view of Raoul and Maria when they left the church.

As the minutes ticked by he began to question his motive in coming to the church. Was it idle curiosity? No, surely it was more than that. He was acquainted with the two who would shortly be leaving the church. Raoul had attended the same school as he had. They had shared the same lessons. They had grown up together. They had fought against each other, in fist-battles which he had invariably won, since Raoul was smaller than him and could not match his strength. Sometimes the fights had been over some girl or other, particularly one girl. It was his younger sister, Carla. He had warned her that Raoul was a thief and a cheat and an unprincipled scoundrel. But the more he had warned her against him, the more she had seemed to be attracted to him. Then came the came the day when he had found the two in a compromising situation in the barn. Raoul had been half-undressed and there were one or two items of Carla's clothing lying about. He hadn't hesitated. He had hit Raoul time and time again. Carla had screamed at him to try to stop him, but he had kept on hitting him. He had only stopped when he had realized that Raoul was unconscious.

Shortly after he had been sent to work on his uncle's farm. Then his father had sold their farm and they had moved to Texas. So he hadn't met

Raoul from the time he had half-killed him until yesterday when Raoul had seen the two of them in the river. Raoul had pretended not to recognize him. But he hadn't fooled Paul for a moment. You don't fail to recognize somebody who beat you up the last time that you met. Even though it had been ten years ago.

His thoughts were jerked back to the present by the door of the church suddenly opening. Raoul and Maria stood there. There was a sharp intake of breath from the hundreds who had been waiting expectantly. They were not disappointed. What they beheld was a beautiful apparition in white. Paul stared at Maria, prying to spot some glimmer of emotion on her face. But her face was as expressionless as the stone angels on the pillars by the sides of the door.

The couple stood in the doorway for several seconds while the crowd stared at them. Raoul was in his army uniform of a general. He stood savouring the admiration of the audience. A couple of times he glanced at his bride. Paul detected a note of proud ownership in his glances.

Paul had seen all he wanted to see. He was about to jump down from the wall when there was a sudden movement in the crowd near the church door. A man pushed his way through. The crowd watched in surprise as the man stepped right up to the couple. The man's next movement took them even more by surprise. He seized Maria around the waist and swept her off her feet. Her scream could be heard all around the front of the church.

The man had started to carry Maria away. He was a big man and held Maria tightly. Her white dress stood out incongruously against his dark clothes. Her captor held her so that the guards standing by the church gates couldn't get a clear shot at him. There was one person however who could get a clear shot. Paul took advantage of the second or two when the Mexican was about forty yards away from him. Paul took careful aim and shot him in the head.

CHAPTER 9

Paul was seated in a room in the church house. Also in the room was Raoul and the priest.

'I must thank you for killing the man who tried to abduct my wife,' said Raoul. 'It was a perfect shot. He died instantly.'

'I'm a soldier in the US Cavalry,' stated Paul. 'I'm trained to shoot accurately.'

Surprise registered on Raoul's face. 'Then you are living in America?'

So this time he wasn't going to pretend that they hadn't been acquainted.

'I've been in America for over ten years,' replied Paul.

The priest was a short middle-aged man with a round face which would usually have a twinkle in the eyes. Now, however, his eyes were troubled.

'I don't usually condone killing,' he stated. 'But in this case I feel that it was justified.'

'How's Maria?' demanded Paul.

'She's in a state of shock,' said the priest. 'The housemaid is attending to her.'

'It's not the ideal way to start a marriage,' said Raoul. 'But I think she's quite resilient. Of course you would know all about that.' He addressed the statement to Paul. 'You two came through the desert together.'

The priest regarded Paul with new interest.

'You two came through the desert together?'

'It was my duty to deliver Maria to Raoul.'

'I would say you've carried it out perfectly. You've not only delivered her, but you've saved her from being kidnapped.'

As if on cue Maria entered the room. She had changed from her wedding-dress and was now wearing a simple black dress.

'Are you all right, dear?' demanded Raoul, with a mixture of concern and pride of ownership in his voice.

'Yes. Thanks to Paul.'

She came over to him and offered her hand. He accepted it gravely and raised it to his lips. Although Maria's face had been expressionless when she had approached him, there was now a hint of a smile on her lips as Paul kissed her hand.

'I'm delighted that you weren't harmed,' he said.

'Of course we will reward Paul for his timely act,' said Raoul.

'There's no need for any reward,' said Paul, quickly. 'To know that Maria is safe is enough of a reward.'

'Why should that man try to abduct her?' asked the priest.

'I'm not exactly sure, but I believe he's one of Luis's men,' said Raoul.

The priest offered them a glass of tequila but Paul refused, saying that he must be on his way. Maria accompanied him to the door. They stood there facing each other for a few moments. Then she kissed him lightly on the lips.

'Be careful, Paul,' she whispered, before turning and going back into the house.

Paul strode the streets, heading for the stable where his horse had been kept. Would this be the last time for him to walk through the town where he had spent so many years when he was younger? Was his parting with Maria the last time he would ever see her? The thought of her being Raoul's wife stuck in his throat. To think of her unique beauty being available for Raoul's pleasure and her body being his to command. He involuntarily quickened his pace to try to banish the thought.

In the stable he haggled with the old man for a saddle. He eventually bought one for three American dollars although the old man had asked ten in the first place. It would probably be his last exercise in haggling. Here it was a way of life. It was expected of every buyer. Over the border in Texas you would automatically pay the asking price without any questions.

He mounted the horse and rode slowly away from the stable. He had filled the water bottles but had no intention of riding through the desert. It was only just past midday and to have one journey through the searing heat was enough for any person. He knew there was an alternative route to the north. It would mean adding another ten miles to his journey, but he was in no hurry. He would still be in time to arrive at Fort Manton before dusk.

He soon left the town behind and was heading for the river. In his mind's eye he could see the last time he had arrived there. He could visualize Maria jumping from her horse and whooping with joy as she splashed the water over herself. He smiled at the thought. She had acted like an excited schoolgirl, far removed from the lady of quality he had left behind in San Caldiz.

His thoughts were interrupted by a sound which was instantly familiar to him. It was the sound of a rifle shot. He instinctively knew that the shot was meant for him. His physical reaction was equally instinctive – he rolled off the saddle, grabbing his rifle from its sheath as he did so.

CHAPTER 10

In Fort Manton Major Linton had a guest in his office. His name was Charles Greer. Like the major, Greer was middle-aged. However he was not dressed in army uniform but in a well-cut grey suit. Everything about him spelled money, from the expensive gold watch in his waistcoat pocket to his diamond signet ring and to the gold cigar-case from which he was offering the major a cigar. The reason for the ostentatious display of wealth was due to the fact that Greer was indeed wealthy. He was the owner of several banks.

The major accepted the cigar. He sniffed it appreciatively. He applied a match to it and puffed contentedly for a few moments. When he was content that it was glowing satisfactorily, he tossed the match away.

'That's one thing I miss in this outpost,' he stated. 'A good cigar.'

'I'll have a regular supply sent to you,' said

Greer, who was also enjoying his cigar.

'Thank you. Of course I will pay for them.'

'There's no need.' Greer waved a dismissive hand. 'You've already contributed enough in other ways.'

'Let's say I've started the ball rolling,' said Linton. He was more than happy with the way the meeting was going. If he had a crystal ball to look into the future he should be able to see an endless succession of boxes of cigars as presents from his wealthy visitor.

'Of course this is a completely new venture,' said Greer. 'Nobody has ever done it before.'

'I suppose that's what makes it so challenging,' stated the major.

'Exactly.' Greer was pleased that Linton had grasped the point. In the first place he had thought of the major as an unimaginative, plodding army officer who was just content to bide his time and wait for his retirement, when he would be enjoying a fairly substantial pension. But he had revised his opinion. It now seemed that the major was as excited by the news as he was. Well, almost as excited. After all, it was his baby, and nobody could be more involved than him. He had been there at the conception and he hoped to be there at the birth. He half-smiled at the thought.

'What about a glass of Scotch whisky to toast the project?' suggested the major.

'An excellent idea,' replied Greer.

The major went over to a cabinet. He produced two glasses and a bottle of whisky.

'Although we don't get the best cigars here, we do at least manage to have a supply of good whisky,' stated the major, as he poured out two generous glasses. 'We get it from an old established firm in Hawkesville. They import it directly from Scotland.'

Greer accepted the glass. Instead of returning immediately to his seat Linton stood for a moment. 'A toast,' he said, raising his glass. 'To the Universal Bank.'

'The Universal Bank,' echoed Greer. He drank some of his whisky. He kept his face expressionless and managed not to betray his thoughts. Well, if the old army dog opposite thought this was good whisky, then he couldn't know anything about whisky. He was already revising his impulsive gesture to send the major some boxes of cigars. He would, of course, keep to his promise, but the cigars wouldn't be the best quality. If the major couldn't recognize good whisky it followed that he wouldn't know a good cigar, although a few minutes ago he had pretended to do so.

'I've already sent the messages you gave me to San Caldiz,' announced Linton. 'They should have arrived there by now.'

'I assume you send them by a reliable courier,' said Greer.

'Oh, yes, his name is Sergeant – er – Captain Callaghan. He has the added advantage of speaking Spanish.'

'He sounds the right man to take my messages to Raoul,' said Greer. 'When I receive an acknowledgment in return I can go ahead to make arrangements to move the money.'

'I expect you will want some of my men as an escort,' stated the major.

'Of course.' Greer smiled. 'Your co-operation will not go unrewarded. If you, or any member of your family, for instance, need a personal loan I will arrange it at nought per cent interest.'

Linton, too, smiled, although his facial response was less than sincere. With all the co-operation he would be giving the bloated moneybag sitting opposite him he could well have given him a cash sum for helping to set up the Universal Bank in San Caldiz.

CHAPTER 11

Paul rolled over in the approved textbook fashion
after hitting the ground. A couple of bullets tried
to halt his progress but they hit the ground near
him. He soon realized however that if he continued rolling over like this one of the bullets could
find its target and hit him instead of the ground.

He fired a bullet from his rifle in the general
direction of his attacker. He knew it wouldn't stop
the attack but he hoped it would give him a split
second in which to assess his situation. His instant
impression was that things didn't look too rosy. He
was out in the open and was really a sitting target
for the rifleman. Or at least a lying-down target,
since he was spread-eagled on the ground. The
only consolation he could find from his position
was that he had identified roughly where the
attacker was hiding. He was concealed behind

some trees. The trees were a couple of hundred yards away. The distance would be no problem to an expert shot. But if the three bullets which had been aimed in his direction were anything to go by, then the gunman was slightly less than a perfect rifleman.

As another bullet tore into the ground a couple of feet away Paul realized that his best hope lay in putting even more distance between himself and the gunman. He put his plan into action. He began to crawl rapidly away from the immediate danger area. He was followed by a succession of bullets, at least two of which were uncomfortably close.

He succeeded in reaching the safety of another stand of trees. He dived gratefully behind them. Another couple of bullets hit the nearby branches, but again they weren't too life-threatening.

My turn now, said Paul to himself, as he steadied his rifle and took aim. He had formed an accurate picture of the whereabouts of the gunman. All he had to do now was to wait.

Whether the gunman thought that he was quite safe, since the distance between him and Paul was too great for accurate shooting, Paul would never know. What he did see was a sudden movement behind the trees. The gunman had obviously decided to change his mode of attack. He slipped between the trees, probably intending to jump on his horse which was grazing somewhere in the background.

It was one more mistake the gunman made. The other mistakes included missing his intended target, Paul, with his succession of bullets. Paul took careful at the gunman as he tried to find the safety of another of the trees. Paul shot him in the head.

Paul waited a few seconds before advancing cautiously to examine the gunman. His assumption was correct that he had shot him in the head. He was a Mexican who had obviously died instantly.

Paul set about the gruesome task of trying to find any identification on him. There wasn't any. The only find of any significance was the surprising amount of money the Mexican had been carrying with him. It consisted of a bundle of American dollars. Paul leafed through them and counted fifty. He stared at the money thoughtfully. They were neatly bundled together. Were they payment for an act to be completed? An act of murder, with the victim being himself. Maybe the would-be assassin had received fifty dollars in advance and would have had another fifty dollars when the deed had been successfully completed. If he was correct then his life would be worth a hundred dollars. Not much, in his consideration. He had always thought that he would have been worth more than that. A thousand dollars at least.

He had no handy spade with which to bury the body. Of course he could leave it to the tender mercies of the vultures. They would pick it clean in a remarkably short while. But although the Mexican had tried to kill him, he felt he couldn't leave him out in the open. He set about finding some stones. He placed the body in a shallow space between two trees. He set about covering him with stones.

It took him longer than he expected. When at last he had finished there was no sign of the body beneath the stones. He gave the makeshift grave one last glance before jumping on his horse and starting out for Fort Manton once more. Who had Maria tried to warn him about? Well, whoever was responsible for the attack, there was no doubt that her warning had been justified. The only reasonable explanation was that the gunman had been one of Luis's men. If he was correct then he had killed two of the outlaw's men in the past two hours. If his popularity with the outlaw had been at a low ebb after the first killing outside the church, then it would definitely be less than zero after the latest episode. His only consolation was that he was unlikely to return to San Caldiz and so give another of Luis's gunmen a chance to take a shot at him.

CHAPTER 12

It was late when Paul eventually arrived at Fort Manton. He was tired and planned to slip into his bed without disturbing the other sergeants who were already sleeping. However his plan was thwarted by a private who was on duty at the living-quarters. He informed him that the major wanted to see him.

'At this hour?' demanded a surprised Paul.

'That's what he said,' retorted the private.

He was even more surprised when he entered the major's office and found him comfortably relaxed and smoking a cigar.

'Ah, sit down, Callaghan.' The officer waved him to a chair. As Paul passed he thought he detected a strong smell of whisky.

Paul sat down. 'I delivered Maria Lopez to the Mayor of San Caldiz as instructed,' said Paul.

'You didn't have any problems?'

'Well, sir, her horse was bitten by a rattler in the desert and I had to shoot it.'

'We won't deduct it out of your wages, the cost of shooting government property.' The major smiled.

He is in a good mood tonight, thought Paul, as he tried to conceal a yawn.

'I don't suppose anything else untoward happened?' enquired his superior officer.

'I shot a Mexican when he tried to kidnap Maria at her wedding,' supplied Paul.

'Well, well, you *were* busy with your rifle. I don't suppose you shot anybody else?'

'Yes, sir, I did. I shot a Mexican who had been tailing me after I left San Caldiz. I believe he's a member of Luis's gang.'

'Who's Luis?' For the first time a frown appeared on the major's face.

'He's the outlaw who tried to kidnap Maria.'

'I see,' said the major, thoughtfully. 'So San Caldiz seems to be a pretty lawless place.'

'No worse than Hawkesville, I would say,' stated Paul.

'Since when are you an authority on the two towns?' the major snapped. His air of *bonhomie* had vanished and been replaced by his more familiar glare when dealing with his subordinates.

'I lived just outside Hawkesville for a few years.

And I went to school in San Caldiz,' said Paul, mildly.

'Yes, I'd forgotten about that.' The major passed a weary hand over his brow.

So he's tired, too, Paul thought, hopefully. Maybe he'll dismiss me in a few moments and I can have a long stay in bed. Surely they'll excuse me any duties tomorrow.

'What about the papers?' demanded the major.

'Wh-at papers?' For a moment he couldn't think what on earth he was talking about.

'The papers I gave you to give to Raoul.' The major spoke slowly and emphasized every word.

Having racked his brains Paul suddenly realized what papers the major meant.

'I'm afraid I lost them in the desert, sir.'

'You lost them in the desert?' His superior officer's voice had suddenly risen a few decibels.

'After Maria's horse had been bitten by a rattler we both had to ride on my horse.'

'I suppose that, too, was bitten by a rattler,' said the major, sarcastically.

'No, sir, it bolted.'

'Let me get this straight. You ended up walking in the desert since you had shot the one horse and the other had bolted.'

'That's right, sir. That's how I came to lose my jacket with the papers inside them.'

'I must be getting old, Callaghan.' The major

passed another weary hand over his brow. 'Given the fact that you were now walking to the Rio Grande, what's it got to do with losing the letters I gave you?'

'I left my jacket in the desert. It was getting pretty hot.'

'You left your jacket in the desert with the letters intended for the Mayor of San Caldiz.' The major uttered the words with the thoughtful air of somebody who had just made an unpleasant discovery. Suddenly his mood changed. 'Do you know what was in those letters?' he shouted out the question.

'No, sir, you didn't tell me,' said Paul, mildly.

'I didn't tell you because I didn't think you were going to lose two horses and do a striptease in the middle of the desert.' The major was still shouting. Paul wisely decided not to say anything, even though he could have corrected the statement by revealing that he had recaptured one of the horses. He had the distinct feeling that to complicate matters by explaining his brush with the Apaches would only bring on another fit of shouting.

'The letters contained information to Raoul about a transfer of money to a bank which he has opened in San Caldiz. The money is being transferred from the Western Universal Bank to Mexico. It is a new venture by the head of the bank, Mr Greer. He was here a couple of hours ago asking me whether everything had been taken care of preparatory to making the smooth transfer of the money possible in a couple of days' time. Like a fool I told him that everything had gone smoothly. I didn't know at the time that I had given the letters to a simpleton who had lost them in the desert.'

'Does this Mr Greer know what he's doing, trusting Raoul with hundreds of dollars to put in his bank in San Caldiz?' demanded Paul. 'Raoul is the biggest crook south of the border.'

'So suddenly you're not only an expert on the two important towns on either side of the border, but also of the status of the crooks in Mexico,' said the major, sarcastically.

'I know all about Raoul. I went to school with him,' stated Paul.

The major stared at him There had been a sharpness in his last remark which hadn't been apparent in his previous answers. Well, whatever was between the sergeant and Raoul was none of his business. His only concern was to get the money, which would be on the wagon in two days' time, to San Caldiz.

'On Friday morning, at daybreak, there will be a wagon starting out from here to cross the desert to get to San Caldiz. There will be gold and dollars on the wagon enough to open a new bank there. Raoul is expecting the delivery, but he doesn't know when it will arrive. Your task is to go back to San Caldiz and tell him exactly when to expect the wagon. Do I make myself clear?'

'I've got to go early in the morning?' Paul was dismayed at the prospect.

'You're getting the picture, Callaghan.' The major looked at his watch. 'If you hurry you should get five hours' sleep.'

Paul turned to leave the office. The major's voice stopped him by the door.

'And Callaghan – if you fail to deliver the message I will personally see to it that your next posting will be to the navy. Where you will be sent on the furthest expedition they can find.'

CHAPTER 13

Paul rode through the desert the following morning without mishap, although on a few occasions he found himself dozing off and just managed to jerk himself awake in time. He arrived at the Rio Grande before midday. This time there was no female companion to jump into the river and splash around like a schoolgirl and no Raoul waiting on the opposite bank. He succeeded in finding Raoul, however, about half an hour later. He had ridden into San Caldiz and headed for the grey stone building which he remembered had once been a castle but had been taken over by the town council many years before.

He was quickly ushered into Raoul's presence after announcing his name. Raoul's office was on a grander scale than the major's in Fort Manton. There was a thick coloured carpet on the floor as distinct from the coconut mats in the major's office. The walls were painted bright yellow instead of army grey. Raol's desk was more imposing than the major's and the chief piece of furniture, a drinks cabinet, also put the major's sideboard to shame.

Raoul stood up to shake his hand.

'What brings you back to San Caldiz so soon?' he demanded.

'I've got a message from Major Linton.' Ordinarily Paul would have refused Raoul's offer of a chair. The less time he spent with the crook the better it would suit him. But he was so weary after his journey and having had only a few hours' sleep the night before, that he accepted the chair.

'Well?' demanded Raoul expectantly.

'The gold and money will be delivered in two days' time.'

'You could have told me that yesterday.'

'I didn't know yesterday,' said Paul, sharply.

'Well, anyway, I know now.'

'It will be delivered in the morning. The wagon will be starting at daybreak.'

Raoul nodded. 'Yes, that makes sense. My men will be waiting at the river. At the usual crossing-point.'

'I'll be joining you. My orders are to see that the wagon gets safely to the bank. Where is it, by the way?'

'It's at the end of Cortez Street. You'd better

report here in the morning and then you can ride out with my men.'

Paul stood up.

'I'll be here.' He left the office. He couldn't get away from it quickly enough. To him there was the smell of corruption about the place. Anything with which Raoul dealt would be corrupt.

Until now he had refrained from dwelling on thoughts of Maria, but having come face to face with her husband the floodgates of his mind were opened. How could she have married such a turd? There couldn't be any feelings of love between them. The only thing he could think of was that it had been a marriage arranged between Maria's father and Raoul. One possibility was that Maria's father owed Raoul money and so he had repaid his debt by sacrificing his daughter's happiness. The idea would be scoffed at in America, where most people were free to make their own choices, but here it was different. Arranged marriages were still the order of the day. Of course Raoul would have jumped at the idea of marrying Maria. To marry the person who was probably the most beautiful woman in Mexico would make him the envy of all men. It would undoubtedly add to his status as mayor of San Caldiz.

He arrived at the stable which he had used the day before. The old man opened the gate and surveyed his horse.

'You brought him in yesterday,' he announced.

'That's right. Look after him for a couple of days. See that he's well fed. If he isn't, the information will be passed on to Raoul.'

There was fear in the old man's eyes at the mention of the mayor's name.

'I'll look after him. I promise.' he said, with a tremor in his voice.

Paul's next call was the lodging-house where he had last spent the night. He knew he could afford to go to a hotel but the lodging-house suited him because it was quiet. He didn't particularly want to mix with people. All he needed at the moment was a bed to enjoy his siesta.

The landlady regarded him with more than a little surprise.

'I thought you'd gone back over the border.'

'I did. But I've come back. I'll have a room for a couple of nights.'

'Would you like some coffee?'

Paul was surprised at the offer. He had assumed that he would have to wait until that evening before sitting down at the dining-table.

'You're the American who shot the bandit at the wedding, aren't you?' she asked, as she poured his coffee.

So that was it. His fame had gone before him.

'Yes, that's me,' said Paul, sipping his coffee.

'I thought it was you,' she said, triumphantly.

Her next statement, however, completely took Paul by surprise.

'Of course you didn't succeed in putting the bandits off kidnapping Maria.'

CHAPTER 14

Later in the day, having enjoyed a surprisingly tasty meal of chicken-soup and tortillas, Paul went out into the street. He had no plans, he just walked aimlessly about. The town was at its best in the evening when the shadows sliced into the buildings and the heat of the day had given way to cooler air. There was more activity on the streets, too. A noticeable change from the early part of the day was that there were now more *señoritas* and young men out on the streets. The girls wore colourful dresses and the young men, as if trying to compete with them, were wearing bright-hued shirts.

As he walked the streets Paul found himself glancing from time to time at the men who were strolling along, some with a female companion. Paul was interested in looking at men who were about his own age. It would be nice to meet one of his old schoolfriends. Even though it was ten years since he'd left there was a good chance that he would recognize them. After all, he had recognized Raoul without any difficulty.

Without his consciously intending it his footsteps led him to the farm where he had spent many happy years. He was surprised at how little it seemed to have changed. There was the same iron gate leading to the garden path. There was the same garden. His father had always kept a good supply of potatoes and other vegetables. Indeed he had provided the four of them with much of the food they needed for most of the year.

He was leaning on the gate surveying the garden and enjoying his memories when a man appeared in the doorway. He was a middle-aged man whose face wore a scowl.

'What are you doing here?' he demanded.

'I'm sorry. I used to live here. I was just thinking about the past,' said Paul.

The man's less than friendly expression didn't change.

'Well you're not welcome now,' he informed Paul.

At that moment a younger version of the man appeared. His expression was more friendly. Indeed it changed first from surprise then to pleasure.

'Paul, is it you?' he demanded.

For a couple of seconds Paul couldn't identify him. Then recollection flooded back.

'It's Sebastian, isn't it?'

'That's right.'

The two shook hands warmly. Sebastian introduced Paul to his father whose expression thawed at the knowledge that Paul had been one of his son's schoolfriends.

'Come in and have a cup of coffee,' said Sebastian.

Paul hadn't intended going into the house, but Sebastian was insistent. Paul went inside where he was introduced to Sebastian's wife. She was a dark-haired, pretty young woman who made them coffee then left them to discuss old times while she went into the kitchen.

'So how long have you lived here?' Paul asked.

'About three years. Your father sold it to a family named the Merinos, then my father bought it from them. So what are you doing in San Caldiz?'

'I'm here on duty for a couple of days. I'm in the American Cavalry.'

'Fancy that,' said his friend, unable to keep the admiration out of his voice. 'I expect you've had some exciting adventures.'

'One or two,' admitted Paul.

'Of course you always were pretty wild,' said Sebastian. 'I remember when you found Raoul with your sister in the barn, you half-killed him.'

'He deserved it,' said Paul. 'She was only four-teen and he was sixteen.'

'Yes, he deserved it,' agreed Sebastian, becom-ing serious. 'Especially after what happened to her.'

'What do you mean?' demanded a puzzled Paul.

'You should know. You were her only brother.'

'A few months after the incident in the barn I was sent to my uncle's farm in Topez. I had finished school and so I spent the rest of the summer helping him. When I came back Carla was dead. My mother said she had had scarlet fever and died.'

'That's not true. She told you that but the truth was that she had had a baby after Raoul had raped her in the barn. The baby was born prematurely. Both the baby and your sister died. Your mother didn't tell you the truth because you would have killed Raoul.'

Paul stood up. His face was white. He stood up gripping the edge of the table.

'Are you sure this is the truth?'

'I'm positive. Ask any of our schoolfriends.'

Paul went towards the door.

'What are you going to do?' demanded Sebastian, who had never seen anyone looking so angry.

'This time I'm going to kill the bastard,' said Paul.

CHAPTER 15

A couple of hours earlier a Mexican had been riding along a narrow mountain path. There was nothing remarkable in that. Many Mexicans grazed their sheep or goats on the mountainside and could be seen from time to time riding along the narrow paths which had been used down the centuries to provide a way of travelling on the mountains. However this Mexican, whose name was Paco, was travelling along the path as quickly as he could. He had no interest in sheep or goats. He was on his way to deliver a message to the bandit, Luis.

As he travelled on his small mountain pony he wondered how much Luis would pay him for the information. It was definitely worth a few dollars. How many should he ask for? He knew that Luis would make him bring his original figure down. So suppose he asked for twenty dollars. Luis would say ten. He would pretend that his lowest figure would be fifteen. Luis would say twelve. Then they would settle on twelve which he could have accepted in the first place. But honour would have been saved.

He had travelled along this mountain road a few times before. He knew it led to Luis's camp. He knew because the soldiers who had returned from the two unsuccessful attempts to wipe out Luis and his followers had told him how to get to the camp. He was glad he was too old to be a soldier because the casualties among Raoul's men had been twice as heavy as those among Luis's. The two battles had undoubtedly been victories for Luis. The only thing which had marred the two victories was that Raoul had managed to survive on both occasions. Rumour had it that the reason he had survived was that he had been behind his soldiers instead of in front of them as was customary with generals.

Paco's horse stumbled on the narrow path. He managed to control it and guide it back to safety. He trembled as he looked down at the drop on the side. If the horse had fallen and he with it, then as sure as there was a heaven above he would have been joining the heavenly host. There was a drop of at least a couple of hundred feet down the mountainside. If he had fallen Luis would never have received the information which he had been hurrying to impart.

He carried on riding, but this time even more

slowly. It seemed to be ages before he spied the outlaw's camp in the distance. At the same time there was the unmistakable *click* of a rifle.

'All right, that's far enough,' said an outlaw as he stepped out from behind a large rock.

'I've got an important message for Luis,' Paco blurted out.

'You can give it to me and save yourself the trouble of riding any further,' said the outlaw.

'It's for Luis, and nobody else,' said Paco, stubbornly. 'It's about Raoul.'

The outlaw studied Paco for a few moments. He obviously decided that Paco's information was only for Luis's ears.

'All right, follow me,' he commanded.

Ten minutes later Paco was led into the camp. He was surprised how many tents there were. He had expected about a dozen at the most. But there seemed to be almost fifty.

They approached the large tent in the centre.

'Wait here,' the outlaw gave the order tersely.

Paco stood uncomfortably outide the tent. He was aware of the curious stares of some of the children who were playing nearby. He glanced around. Outside one of the other tents a small group of women were washing some clothes in a large tub. They, too, stared at Paco with interest.

After what seemed an endless time but was probably only a couple of minutes, Luis appeared. He was dressed in his full major's uniform. He gave Paco the sort of searching stare he would have given any of his soldiers on parade.

'You've got a message for me?' he snapped.

'Yes. I work for Raoul in the mayor's office.'

'So?'

'I know that he is expecting a special delivery the day after tomorrow.'

'Go on.'

'At his bank.'

Luis's face showed a flicker of interest for the first time.

'Are you sure?'

'I'm positive. I overheard the conversation between him and the American cavalry soldier.'

'I want to know the details.'

'It will cost you.'

'How much.'

'Twenty dollars. American.'

To Paco's surprise Luis didn't demur. He produced a wallet and counted out twenty American dollars in notes. Although Paco was amazed at the instant payment he managed to keep a straight face. His voice, too, was steady as he informed Luis about the time of the expected delivery of gold and notes to Luis's bank.

'You say they will be delivered about midday and the carriage bringing the consignment will be coming through the desert?'

'That's right,' said Paco, pocketing his money. For a second he had taken his eyes off Luis's face as he carefully put the notes in his wallet. It was long enough for Luis to draw his revolver with lightning speed and shoot Paco in the heart.

'Get my money back for me, will you?' he asked one of the guards casually.

CHAPTER 16

Paul was walking the streets. Whereas an hour before he had been strolling casually through the town idly taking in the sights, now he was striding through the streets bursting with anger.

The bastard! The rat! The swine!

To think that a few hours ago Raoul had welcomed him into his office, not exactly with warmth but as an old acquaintance. Yet all the time Raoul had been harbouring the guilty secret that he had raped Carla and been responsible for her death. No, that wasn't right. Someone like Raoul wouldn't know anything about guilt. His kind of mentality wouldn't admit that they had ever done anything wrong. If he did he would be spending most of his life in church confessing his sins to the priest.

Paul's blind anger had led him to the grey building which he had entered that morning. It was now closed for the day but he found himself glancing involuntarily up at the window which he knew looked out of Raoul's office. Indeed he stood so long staring at the window that some of the passers-by glanced at him curiously. He was unaware of their interest in the tall American who was staring so fixedly at the old castle. It was while Paul was staring at the mayor's office that the unexpected happened. A plan suddenly came to him.

He examined it as he walked back to his lodgings. This time he was walking slowly. His anger had been replaced by excitement. The more he examined the plan, the more foolproof it seemed.

His landlady was surprised when Paul returned early to the house. He had obviously become a minor celebrity after shooting one of Luis's men outside the church. She was sitting down to a cup of coffee and offered him one.

'It's a pity about the young lady ,' she observed as she poured his cup.

'What's this outlaw, Luis, like?' demanded Paul.

'They say he's a bigger crook than Raoul. He gets his money to pay his outlaws from the poppy fields.'

'So he's into the opium trade,' said Paul, thoughtfully.

'So they say. Of course the fields are a long way away, but Luis gets his supply along the mountain trails.'

'Some of the opium is being sold to our soldiers,' stated Paul.

'Luis sells some of it here in San Caldiz. It's not too difficult to get hold of.'

Paul finished his drink. 'Thanks for the coffee. I'll be off early in the morning.'

'Will you be coming back here?'

'Yes, that's the plan,' said Paul.

The following morning he set off across the desert. This is getting a regular journey, he though, mirthlessly, as he headed north. However the ride didn't trouble him. He was used to spending long hours in the saddle. One of the tests which he had been forced to undergo before he had been accepted into the cavalry was that he had to ride thirty miles. Unlike many of the other trainees he had enjoyed the task. Ever since, time spent in the saddle hadn't been a problem. In fact he welcomed it on some occasions. He found that the constant movement helped to banish any unwelcome thoughts from his mind.

At the moment these thoughts centred on Raoul. There was no doubt that Raoul deserved to die. And he, Paul, was the obvious person to carry out the execution. If Raoul hadn't raped Carla there was a possibility that his lovely sister would be alive today. The mistake he had made was in not killing Raoul when he had beaten him unconscious in the barn. But he would be able to put the record straight tomorrow. If Raoul did but know it he had only twenty-four hours to live.

He went over his plan. Yes, it certainly seemed foolproof. The beauty of it was that Raoul would be killed and he would not be held accountable. The last thing he wanted would be to be hanged for killing Raoul.

At last the fort stood out on the horizon. He rode towards it steadily. The sun was now bearing down on him. He would be glad to get out of its glare and into the cool shade of the fort.

Within ten minutes of his arrival he was ushered into the presence of Major Linton.

'Shouldn't you be in San Caldiz, Callaghan?' was the major's greeting.

'I'm afraid there's been a hitch in the plans for tomorrow,' said Paul.

'What do you mean – a hitch?' said the major, visualizing his supply of expensive cigars rapidly disappearing.

'Well, it's only a minor one,' Paul hastened to inform him.

'Right, let's hear this minor problem.'

'Raoul has been deposed.'

'Raoul deposed? That seems like a major problem to me.' His supply of cigars had by now completely disappeared.

'His deputy, Manuel, has replaced him. Nothing, however, has changed. The soldiers will be arriving to take charge of the money as arranged.'

'I can't hand over Greer's money to anybody except Raoul,' said the major, angrily.

'That's where my plan comes in,' said Paul. 'I'll be accompanying Manuel to the change-over place at the edge of the river. Our soldiers will be on the other side. I will point out Manuel by touching him on the shoulder. The men will shoot him. Raoul will be restored as the rightful mayor and everything will proceed as planned.'

'Mm.' The major gave the plan some thought. In fact he gave it quite a lot of thought. Paul didn't know it, but if it wasn't for the cigars the major would have dismissed the plan out of hand. After all, the arrangement was to hand over the money to Raoul, not to some upstart named Manuel. What did they know about this Manuel? Not that it mattered much if his sergeant's plan were to succeed. It was a simple plan. The kind which could come off. Anyhow he had an alternative plan, assuming that for some reason this Manuel wasn't killed. The money wouldn't have been handed over. His men would still be on their own side of the river. All they would have to do would be to turn round and come back to the fort.

Paul was waiting impatiently for the major's reply. It was obviously going to be touch-and-go whether his superior officer accepted his plan or not. If he did not agree to it, the only alternative would be to go back and try to kill Raoul himself. The difficulty was that Raoul was so well protected by his guards that it would be almost impossible to get near to him. That was why his plan seemed such a perfect one. To get the sharpshooters in the cavalry to kill Raoul would solve everything.

'Hrrumph.' The major cleared his throat. Paul knew it was a preliminary to making an important announcement.

'Against my better judgement, I've decided to go along with your plan, Callaghan. Captain Bingley will be in charge. Before you go back to San Caldiz later today there will be a meeting here of the three of us. There's no need for me to inform you that the plan must have the utmost secrecy. You will not divulge a word to anyone.'

'I swear I won't, sir,' said Paul, trying to keep his overwhelming feeling of exhilaration out of his voice.

CHAPTER 17

When Maria awoke she felt as though she had slept for a week. Now, even though she had opened her eyes, she felt that she was not fully awake. Her head felt woolly and she seemed to have difficulty in focusing on things. She tried to concentrate on the tent-pole, but for some inexplicable reason there seemed to be two instead of one. Then, when she kept her gaze on them, they merged together. Yes, that was better, it was one again.

A tent-pole? What was she doing in a tent? She sprang up from the straw mattress on which she was lying. Straight away her head started playing tricks again. She started to see double. The water-jug which stood in the corner of the tent had suddenly acquired a twin.

Perhaps she was ill; that was why she had suddenly felt giddy when she had sat up in bed. She felt her forehead. No, it didn't seem hot, in fact it felt quite cool. She knew that her heart was racing, but that wasn't surprising considering the shock of suddenly finding herself lying in a strange bed in a strange tent.

A middle-aged woman entered the tent.

'Ah, you're awake. I thought you'd been given too much, and maybe you weren't going to wake up at all.'

'Too much what?' demanded a thin voice. Was it hers?

'Too much opium. By the way, my name's Rosita. You don't have to tell me yours, I already know it.'

'Why was I drugged?' demanded Maria, although she felt she already knew the answer.

'Why, to keep you quiet, of course. You were carried on horseback along the mountain track. The last thing Luis wanted was for you to kick up a fuss while you were being brought here.'

There were several questions buzzing around in her head but somehow the muzziness prevented her from identifying them. One, however, stood out.

'Why did Luis bring me here?'

'Don't you know anything about the feud between Raoul and Luis?'

'I've been abroad for a few years. In France.' Why did she have to sound so apologetic about it?

'Well, Luis and Raoul have been rivals for the past few years. Luis was Mayor of San Caldiz until a couple of years ago. Then Raoul took over the town. He waited until Luis and the rest of the town council were on a hunting expedition up here in the mountains. They were hunting wild boars – not that they caught any. Well, anyway, while they were up here Raoul and his soldiers took over the town. When Luis tried to regain the town they were beaten in a pitched battle. Since then Luis and his supporters have been living up here in the mountains. He's tried to get Raoul to come up here and fight him. But Raoul has led his soldiers up here twice and they've been beaten. There's no way that Raoul would come up here a third time. He'd lose so much face that he wouldn't be able to keep his position as mayor any longer.'

'So I'm the bait to get Raoul to come up the mountain a third time?' demanded Maria, bitterly.

'That's right, dear. Now would you like something to eat. I've got a lovely rabbit-stew in my tent; if you want to come over to have some, you're welcome.'

Although her head still wasn't right, Maria discovered there was nothing wrong with her stomach as she wolfed down a second helping of the stew in Rosita's tent.

When she had finished Luis materialized through the door. Maria guessed his identity from the fact that he was wearing the army uniform of a major.

'It's nice to see that you've been eating, my

dear,' he stated. 'By the way, I'm Luis.'

'I guessed as much,' said Maria, shortly.

'I will be your future husband.'

'But I've already got a husband,' she protested.

'You don't understand. I said *future* husband.'

'You mean after you've killed Raoul?'

'You're getting the picture. I would say that Raoul has got just over a day to live. After that he will be dead and I will be restored to my rightful position of mayor of San Caldiz.'

'You're taking a lot for granted, aren't you?'

'About your compliance? Oh, that's no problem. You are mine from now on and you will do exactly as I tell you.'

He turned on his heel and left.

'You made him angry,' Rosita announced.

'Listen, Rosita,' said Maria, urgently. 'I've got to get away from this place. Where will I be able to steal a horse?'

'You'll never get away,' said Rosita, positively. 'There's only one path out of here. And it's guarded night and day by Luis's guards. I'm afraid you'll have to go through with Luis's plans. After all, you were going to be Raoul's bride. I don't suppose there's much difference in being Luis's wife. You'll still be living like a lady.'

'In a castle tower,' said Maria, bitterly.

CHAPTER 18

Paul's ride back to San Caldiz had been uneventful. Before leaving the fort he had attended the meeting held with the major and Captain Bingley. Paul's plan had been outlined to Bingley. It had taken him some time to grasp the situation, a fact which wasn't surprising to Paul since he didn't have much faith in Bingley's mental powers. In Paul's opinion Bingley was one of the 'yes, sir, three bags full' coterie. Which was how he had managed to obtain his promotion.

'I want three of the best sharpshooters you've got aiming at Raoul,' said Paul, finally.

'You said Raoul,' Bingley pointed out.

'I mean Manuel,' said Paul, quickly. 'He's taking Raoul's place.'

Bingley threw him a suspicious glance.

Apart from that one slight slip-up everything had gone smoothly. Now all he could hope was that tomorrow everything would go equally smoothly. Before he went to sleep that night his thoughts turned to Maria. Where was she now? Somewhere up in the mountains as far as he knew. Well at least she was safe from the clutches of Raoul at the moment.

The following morning Paul awoke after spending a restless night. He had had a dream in which he saw a square with hundreds of people waiting expectantly for something to happen. The expected event was revealed when Paul realized that the crowd were waiting for an execution. The scene was not in America but in Paris. Not a hanging, this execution was to be by the guillotine – a method of execution which Paul had seen in the illustrated books. For a while he was unable to identify the person who was due to have his head chopped off. He had assumed that it would be Raoul, since he was going to die shortly. But when the picture became clearer he was shocked to discover that the person whose head was waiting to be chopped off was him. He awoke in a cold sweat.

Did the dream have any significance? Was it trying to tell him something? Like the fact that it wasn't Raoul who would die today, but himself. He tried to dismiss it. Although he partly succeeded he found that he couldn't go back to sleep again. It was with relief that he heard the cock crow. It was now time for him to get up and see that the right person was executed today – Raoul.

When he went downstairs he found that the

landlady was already busy cooking in the kitchen. He asked for some water to shave. She told him that when he had finished there would be some hot tortillas waiting for him. He really was getting special treatment, he reflected, as he glanced in the mirror in his room while preparing to shave.

The face that stared back at him wasn't too bad. Some women had even considered it quite handsome. It had survived twenty-five years without being marked by the pox, as were some of his fellow soldiers. He wondered what the reaction in the sergeants' mess would be if they learned that he had set up a trap for Raoul. The result of the trap would be that Raoul would be executed today – by a firing squad of the Eleventh Cavalry. It was quite apt. If Raoul were ever brought to account in San Caldiz for his numerous crimes he would be executed by a firing squad here in the town. Instead of which Paul's fellow cavalrymen would be doing the job for them.

He had assumed that he would have little appetite for breakfast. But the smell of the tortillas made him change his mind. He accepted the plateful gratefully.

'It's a good thing for a man to have a healthy appetite,' observed his landlady as he wolfed down the tortillas.

Why did the thought *the condemned man ate a hearty meal* come to him? He wasn't the one who was condemned to death today. It was Raoul. To change the subject he asked the landlady about her other guests.

'Oh, the married couple are still here. But they spend most of their time in bed.' She cackled with laughter.

'What about the other man? The skinny little man?'

'Didn't you hear? He was caught picking pockets. On Raoul's orders he's due to be executed in the square tomorrow.'

Although there were still a few tortillas left on his plate, somehow the news put Paul off eating any more.

CHAPTER 19

Luis and his outlaws too were up early. The second in command, an outlaw named Savales, was summoned to his tent. Savales had a scarred face, the result of being disfigured when his wife had thrown hot fat from a pan at him. They said that his screams of pain could be heard several streets away. He had been tended by an aunt and uncle. When he had recovered sufficiently he had returned home. He had pulled out his knife and stabbed his wife twenty times. That day his revenge had been secured, but the ugly scars on the side of his face would last for ever.

There was one chair in the tent. Luis was sitting in it, so Savales was forced to stand.

'We'll be ready to go in an hour,' said Luis. 'It's about three hours' march to the river. We should be there in plenty of time to prepare our ambush.'

'How many men are we taking?' demanded Savales.

Luis frowned. He didn't like the word 'we'. *He* was the person in charge. Savales had been getting too big for his boots lately. If he weren't careful he wouldn't just be filling his boots but a grave on the mountainside.

'I want every available man.'

'We should be able to muster forty,' said Savales.

There was that 'we' again. If Savales kept on using it he would definitely be shortening his life.

'Forty. Yes, I think I can manage to beat Raoul with forty men. Of course I'll have the element of surprise on my side.'

'I suppose the Americans will be crossing the river at the usual crossing place.'

'It's where they cross the river when they bring supplies to San Caldiz. It's a spot well sheltered by trees. This will give us a hiding-place where we can wait until Raoul has taken charge of the money. When he has, we will attack. Before Raoul's soldiers know what has happened we will have wiped them out. Pass the order that I want Raoul for myself. I, personally, want the pleasure of killing him.'

Raoul, too, had been awake early. Today was going to be a great day for him and he wanted to savour every minute of it. He was shaved by his valet who also brushed his uniform. When Raoul donned it he realized, not for the first time, that it was getting tight on him. This easy life which he had been indulging in lately meant that he had been putting on weight. It was the result of sitting behind his desk for most of the day. He resolved that when he had put all the American's money in his bank he would have his tailor measure him for another suit. A size bigger next time.

All that money – the thought stayed in his mind the way pleasant thoughts sometimes do. With all the money he would probably be the richest man in Mexico. No, the second richest man, since the president would be the richest. He had been seven years in power and would surely have amassed a fortune by giving favours and asking for payment in return. But even the President of Mexico didn't own a bank.

He wondered whether Mr Greer, who owned the Western Alliance Bank, would be accompanying the money to see that it was all transferred correctly to him. Maybe he should have asked Callaghan. Well, anyhow, he should be here shortly, he could ask him then.

When he thought of Callaghan a frown appeared on his face. Callaghan was the fly in the ointment. He would have preferred to be dealing with any other cavalry officer than Callaghan. Years ago he had seduced Callaghan's sister, Carla.

She hadn't exactly been a willing partner to their lovemaking and it had been unfortunate that her brother had turned up when he did. Of course he had hardly been in a position to defend himself. He had taken the mother of all beatings. The first outcome of the episode was that Carla had become pregnant and the second result was that he had sworn that if he ever came across Callaghan again he would kill him for the humiliation he had suffered that day.

He hadn't really believed that he would meet him again. But, by a miracle, Callaghan had been delivered into his town. He prided himself that so far he hadn't revealed his real hatred of the American cavalry sergeant. But, with only a few hours to go, he would soon be in a position to have his revenge. Yes, Callaghan would pay for the beating which he had inflicted on him. He would pay forty times over for every blow he had received that day ten years before.

CHAPTER 20

Maria was aware of the activity going on in the tents around. She put her head out of her own tent and saw that many of the outlaws had gathered in the space outside Luis's tent. They were checking their rifles and ammunition. Something big was in the air. She waited impatiently for Rosita to come into the tent so that she could find out what it was.

When Rosita did at last appear it was obvious that she was bursting to inform her of what was happening.

'There's going to be a big battle,' she announced excitedly.

'Between Luis's men and Raoul's army?'

'That's right.'

'Up here in the mountain?'

'No. Down by the tiver. The Rio Grande.'

'Why are they going to have a battle by the river?'

Rosita sat on the edge of the bed next to her. 'It seems that Raoul is having gold and money brought over from Fort Manton. He's having it to open a new bank in San Caldiz.'

'And Luis aims to stop him?'

'That's right. They say it's going to be the mother and father of all battles.'

'How many men will Luis have?'

'I'm not sure. I think I heard somebody say forty.'

'Knowing Raoul I'd say he'd have a hundred soldiers. So the odds would be on Raoul.'

'But Luis will be able to surprise them. So that must make him the favourite to win the battle.'

'Maybe,' said Maria.

Outside the tent there were the sounds of orders being shouted. It was obvious that the outlaws were preparing to move. A few shots were fired. Luis's voice could be heard. Maria guessed that the shots were fired in excitement rather than at any particular target when she heard Luis shout:

'Save your bullets, you fools. The next person who fires his rifle, will get a bullet from me in the head.'

The next time Maria heard Luis's voice was when he appeared in the tent doorway.

'I see that you're listening with interest to our preparations.' He addressed the remark to Maria.

'I can't help hearing them,' she replied.

'Today I'm going to win a great victory over Raoul,' he boasted.

'I expect Raoul will have something to say about that.'

'When I come back Raoul will be dead. You will no longer be his wife. I will therefore claim you for my own.'

'I'd prefer to be a widow.'

'You won't have any choice,' he snapped, angrily. 'You will obey my commands.'

On the bed Rosita grasped Maria's hand tightly to try to prevent her from uttering another reply which would increase Luis's anger further.

'Yes, my beauty,' said Luis. 'We will make a handsome pair when we ride into San Caldiz together and I will claim what is rightfully mine.'

He stared thoughtfully at Maria. Suddenly he reached across and grabbed her hand. 'A general usually expects a kiss from his future wife before going into battle.'

He pulled her up. Holding her close he planted a kiss on her lips. She didn't struggle. She stood there passively while he kissed her.

When he broke away, he said: 'The next time we kiss I'll expect a more passionate response from you. Or you will feel the weight of my fist.'

He stalked out of the tent.

'What a horrid man,' Maria gasped.

'Sh, he might hear you,' warned Rosita.

'I don't care,' said Maria. 'I wouldn't marry him if he were the last man on earth. I'd kill myself first.'

Outside, more orders were shouted. There were the sounds of horses moving off. There was the sound of cheering as some of the wives and girl-friends wished the outlaws success in the battle to come.

Rosita put her head out through the tent-flap and Maria joined her. Rosita waved to some of the outlaws as they passed by.

'They should have music to send them on their way,' said Maria. 'They should have drums and pipes.'

'If they're successful they'll be marching through San Caldiz soon with a brass band,' supplied Rosita.

'They're not going to win. They won't stand a chance against Raoul,' said Maria.

'I'm not going to argue with you,' Rosita replied stubbornly.

'No, don't let's quarrel,' said Maria. 'Because I'll want your help to escape from this place.'

They had gone back inside the tent.

'Are you mad?' demanded Rosita. 'There's only one path out of here. And as you know, it's guarded.'

'But is it?' demanded Maria. 'Luis has taken all the able-bodied men he could muster to fight his battle. The chances are the path isn't guarded.'

Rosita received the statement in silence.

'You know I could be right,' persisted Maria.

'It's possible,' admitted Rosita, cautiously.

'So all we do is walk around as if we're just stretching our legs. Then we slip out along the path. If the guard is there then we'll have to come back. But if he isn't we carry on walking. I'll pay you well,' she concluded, coaxingly.

'I don't know,' Rosita hesitated.

'You've got a family in San Caldiz, haven't you?'

'Yes, I've got a brother and five sisters.'

'I'm sure you'd prefer to live down in the warm town rather up here in the cold mountains.'

'How much will you pay me?' demanded Rosita.

'Twenty dollars,' replied Maria.

Rosita took a deep breath. 'All right, I agree.'

'Then let's go,' said Maria. 'The sooner we start the better.'

CHAPTER 21

At a safe distance from Fort Manton a couple of dozen or so Apaches had watched with interest the departure of the wagon containing the money intended for Raoul's bank. Originally there had only been three of them but during the past twenty-four hours their numbers had increased steadily. What would have been worrying for the soldiers if they had spotted the Apaches was that they were all wearing war paint. A certain sign that they were on the warpath.

Their visit to the fort started when the three Apaches who had met Paul and Maria in the desert had headed for the fort with the best of intentions. They had found Paul's jacket in the desert. He Who Always Knows Best had announced that the jacket would be worth several dollars if they returned it to the officer in Fort Manton.

'How much do you think we will get for it?'

enquired Eyes Like a Hawk.

'It must be worth at least five dollars,' was the reply. He Who Always Knows best held up the jacket as if by doing so he would be able to gauge its true value.

'We'll take it to Fort Manton,' said Lion in the Hills, who didn't intend letting Eyes Like a Hawk usurp his rights as a leader, even though his keen eyesight had spotted the jacket in the first place.

They rode up to the fort. When Lion in the Hills announced that they wanted to see the captain in charge, the sentry at the gate regarded them with suspicion.

'We don't let Indians in the fort,' was the sharp retort.

'We've got something important for the captain,' replied Lion in the Hills.

'He's a major, not a captain,' replied the guard. 'Wait here,' he added.

In fact they were kept waiting for ages. If it were not that they had developed a stoicism about their dealings with the white man over the years they would have become irritated at the long wait. Instead they accepted it as part of their daily contact with those who had usurped their territory.

Eventually the guard returned.

'The major will see you,' he announced.

They were led into Major Linton's office.

'What can I do for you?' Linton demanded in tones which had more than a little of suspicion in them.

'We've brought you this,' said Lion in the Hills, holding up Paul's jacket.

The major didn't recognize it immediately.

'Where did you get it?' he demanded.

'I found it in the desert,' stated Eyes Like a Hawk.

The major was now examining it. 'It's Callaghan's,' he said, half to himself.

'He's the soldier who stole our horse,' said Lion in the Hills. He didn't add that they had later managed to reclaim it.

'There were two people in the desert. A man and a woman,' said He Who Always Knows Best. 'They took our water bottles.'

Major Linton came to a decision.

'I don't know anything about your horse and the water bottles. For all I know you could be telling lies. But you've brought this jacket back. So you'll have three dollars for it. One each. I think that's fair.'

He was met with blank stares. The trouble with Indians, he later informed one of his sergeants, is that you never know what they are thinking.

The three were given a dollar each by a corporal and they were escorted from the fort.

'I thought we'd get five dollars for it,' said a

disappointed Lion in the Hills.

'Perhaps you should have asked for five dollars,' said He Who Always Knows Best.

'Don't be stupid,' came the reply. 'You don't bargain with the white man. You take what they have to offer.'

It was when they were about to mount their horses in order to ride away from the fort that they made an interesting discovery. They noticed that a carriage had arrived at the fort while they had been inside being questioned by the major. Two soldiers were unloading a heavy chest from the carriage. The soldiers were struggling under its weight and so didn't observe the interest their activity had aroused in the three Apaches. When the soldiers had disappeared inside the building carrying their heavy weight the three watchers hadn't moved a muscle.

A few minutes later the soldiers reappeared. The remark made by one of them was going to trigger a series of events which the soldier couldn't possibly have foreseen.

'I'm glad we're not the ones who will be carrying that box out again tomorrow morning,' he stated.

CHAPTER 22

On a path a couple of hundred yards from Luis's camp Maria was struggling with a guard. Rosita was watching the struggle with horror. There was nothing she could do to help her companion since the path was so narrow.

Maria had been congratulating herself on having escaped from the camp unnoticed. This was probably largely due to the fact that the women who had been left behind after the departure of the outlaws had preferred to seek the privacy of their own tents, rather than mix socially with their neighbours. They had started on their trek along the path which would lead to freedom when disaster struck. The guard had stepped out from behind the rock.

He had seized Maria.

'Where do you think you are going, my pretty maid?' he demanded.

Maria tried to get out of his grasp. When she didn't succeed she said, hoarsely:

'I'll give you money. I'll give you twenty dollars if you'll let me go.'

'It won't be any good to me if I'm dead,' he retorted, 'because Luis will surely kill me if I let you pass.'

Maria began struggling again. There was one slight advantage in her position – the guard didn't have a gun. In all probability all the guns had been commandeered to accompany the outlaws in their coming battle. Maria also realized that the guard was in fact a fairly old man – all the young men presumably being on their way to fight Raoul.

The knowledge that he was quite an old man gave her added strength. When she had been in Paris she had kept herself in trim with swimming, fencing, and whatever other sports a young lady was expected to follow. Her assailant was already beginning to breathe heavily in his efforts to control her violent struggle.

'Keep still,' he cried, as desperately he tried to hold her.

Maria knew that the more she struggled the weaker the old man would become. She redoubled her efforts to tire him. As they struggled they came nearer to the edge of the path. Below lay a drop of several hundred feet. The old man changed his tactic.

'If you don't stop struggling I'll push you over the edge,' he cried.

If he thought this would deter Maria he had completely misread her character. His threat only gave her added strength. In the beginning he had picked her up bodily, thinking he would be able to carry her back to the camp where he would undoubtedly be able to call on help to restrain her. But the effort of keeping her off the ground had soon proved too much because of her constant struggling. He had abandoned that strategy in favour of merely trying to hold her tightly in his arms.

Now as they struggled they veered dangerously close to the edge of the path. Maria struggled to keep her balance while her attacker seemed intent on carrying out his threat of pushing her over the edge. As he tried to control her he swore at her.

They seemed to have been struggling for ages, although it was probably only a couple of minutes. The old man's grip on Maria slipped. With one supreme effort she managed to break away from his grasp. Her assailant gave a roar of frustration as he dived towards her. He had forgotten how near the edge they were. His roar changed to a scream of horror as he went over the edge.

Maria and Rosita clung to each other for several minutes after the outlaw had disappeared over the edge. Maria had plucked up courage to look down to see where he lay. But he was a couple of hundred feet below and from the unnatural position of his body on the rocks it would be safe to assume that he was dead. Rosita couldn't bring herself to look over the edge at the body.

Eventually they broke apart.

'Come on,' said Maria. 'It's all over now.'

'I'll light a candle for him in the church,' said Rosita.

'It was touch-and-go whether it would have been me you'd have been lighting it for,' replied Maria.

CHAPTER 23

When Paul arrived at the council offices he was ushered quickly into the mayor's room. To his surprise Raoul greeted him warmly.

'We've got plenty of time,' said Raoul. 'We'll have a cup of coffee before we set off.'

While an assistant was preparing the coffee, Raoul started talking about the changes which had taken place in San Caldiz.

'Of course you left the town several years ago . . .'

'Ten,' said Paul, shortly.

'Yes, well, during those years we've improved the town a great deal.' He accepted his coffee from the assistant who had handed another cup to Paul. 'We've put in a new water system. We had to lay hundreds of miles of pipes to do so. I think it would be fair to say that we've modernized San Caldiz and it can compare with most towns over the border for its facilities. Of course, the one thing that's been lacking up until now is an international bank. That of course will be remedied today, when we receive the money which your soldiers will be bringing.'

Why was Raoul telling him this? The mayor was treating him as though he were an important visitor to the town whom he was trying to impress. He knew all about the improvements in the town. He begrudgingly admitted that the water system was a big improvement on what it had been when he was a boy. Raoul's next remark took him equally by surprise.

'What do you think you will do after the money has been handed over?'

'I assume I'll go back with the rest of the regiment,' said Paul, guardedly.

'I've got a proposition,' said Raoul. 'No, hear me out,' he continued as Paul began shook his head. 'It's this. Why don't you stay in San Caldiz – at least for a few days? My wife, Maria, has been captured by the outlaw, Luis, as you know. After the transfer of the money I'll be mustering my soldiers and we'll be marching to Luis's camp. It goes without saying that a trained American soldier like yourself would be invaluable in such a conflict. I could even consider making you the leader of the expedition.'

'I believe you've tried twice to defeat Luis without success,' said Paul, drily.

Raoul flushed. For the first time since he had entered the office the mayor showed signs of losing control of his emotions.

Paul hesitated. One part of the suggestion was certainly tempting – the possibility of seeing the beautiful Maria again. Of course, if Raoul was killed as he had planned, then Maria would be a widow. This would allow another man – himself for instance – to be considered as a suitor. He sighed. What point was there in dreaming? Maria wouldn't consider him as a prospective husband. The fact that they had spent several interesting hours in the desert didn't qualify him as a possible lover.

Raoul assumed that Paul's hesitation was due to his giving his suggestion serious thought. If Paul would come on their next venture to kill Luis then it would certainly be an advantage for his soldiers to have a marksman of Paul's calibre accompanying them. Then, having disposed of Luis in the battle it would be the ideal opportunity for him to dispose of Paul. With dozens of bullets flying around the place, one of them could easily accidentally find Paul's head. Then the age-old humiliation would be avenged.

'My soldiers are gathered in the courtyard at the back of the building,' said Raoul. 'Maybe you'd like to inspect them before you make up your mind.'

Paul wasn't keen on inspecting the soldiers, but he wanted to get away from Raoul's office with all its trappings of his power. He agreed to inspect the soldiers.

They were standing at ease when Paul and Raoul arrived in the courtyard. Paul took a quick inventory and guessed that there must be over a hundred. Raoul introduced Paul as an American cavalry officer. He added that Paul might be thinking of joining the regiment.

The sergeant called the parade to attention. He lined them up ready for Paul's inspection. When he had been a captain, before his demotion, Paul had regularly inspected the soldiers under him on parade. Now he went along the ranks slowly as he had often done then.

At the end of the inspection he marched back to join the sergeant and Raoul.

'Well?' demanded Raoul, with pride in his voice. 'What do you think of them?'

'Most of them haven't cleaned their guns for days,' said Paul. 'A soldier's best friend is his rifle. If they're going to take on Luis then they'll want to make sure that their rifles are in perfect working order.'

Raoul scowled. His idea of getting Paul to inspect the soldiers had backfired. Well, his other idea of getting rid of Paul certainly wouldn't be a failure. He would forget about trying to get Paul to come on the trail with them to Luis's camp. He resolved to go back to his original plan and get rid of Paul at the earliest opportunity.

CHAPTER 24

The Apaches were also thinking about rifles. But these were not rifles to be cleaned, these were brand-new rifles.

Lion in the Hills had taken over the role of leader of the war party. After all, he was the leader of the group who had originally discovered the valuable commodity in the trunk. He and the other two had summoned the rest of the war party by the method which they had used for centuries – by smoke signals. The soldiers in the camp had, of course, seen the signals but had attached little importance to them. After all, the Apaches hadn't been any trouble for the past ten years – apart from stealing the odd horse.

If they had had someone in the camp who could read the smoke signals they would have been shocked by what they had discovered. The signals were for a gathering of a war party. The only disadvantage from the Apaches' point of view was that there was little time to gather together a full war party. The number they now had was considerably less than Lion in the Hills would have wanted. Still, they were all young warriors who were anxious to flex their muscles. Also they were all armed, although some only had the traditional bow and arrow. But he had promised them guns and the promise had helped to make them form the war party.

Before they set off on their journey across the desert, Lion in the Hills had delivered the kind of speech with which he imagined the great Geronimo would have inspired his followers.

'Fellow Apaches,' he began. 'Today will be a glorious day in our history. Our exploits will be handed down from generation to generation. Children at their mother's knees will gaze in awe as the story of our success today is recalled . . .'

'Oh, get on with it,' said He Who Always Knows Best.

Lion in the Hills glared at him. He would never forgive him for interrupting him when he had a chance to make the only speech he would probably ever make in his life.

'Yes, you'd better get on with it,' added one of the Apaches, who had recently joined the three. 'Or the soldiers will be so far in front of us that we won't be able to catch them up.'

Lion in the Hills conceded that this was a valid point.

'Well, the three of us ...' he was forced to include He Who Always Knows Best in this triangle although it went against the grain to do so, 'we found out that the soldiers would be loading the most precious commodity we know on to their wagon this morning.'

'What is the most precious commodity?' asked one of the younger Apaches.

'Why, guns,' exclaimed Lion in the Hills. 'What else would they be sending to Mexico? What else could be so heavy? We watched the two soldiers unloading them yesterday. They were big, muscular soldiers and they could hardly carry them into the barracks.'

'Guns.' Several of the Apaches whispered the word as if hardly believing that it could be true.

'From the weight of the chest I would say that there should be thirty guns in it.' said Lion in the Hills.

'Fifty,' stated He Who Always Knows Best.

It was obvious to the assembled warriors that their leader could barely control his temper.

'Well however many are in there they will enhance our lives. They will ensure that we have enough guns to gather a raiding-party three times the size of this. Think what we could achieve with that.'

'The important thing,' said He Who Always Knows Best, 'is that there are only a dozen soldiers accompanying the wagon. There are twice as many of us. So when we come to the river, where the change-over will obviously take place, we will be able to surprise them. When they see us in our war-paint I don't think they'll fight. They won't want to die defending guns intended for the Mexicans. They will leave the guns and take to their heels. We will then step in and take charge of the wagon. Are there any questions?'

There were none.

At a signal from Lion in the Hills they began to ride forward swiftly.

'I was going to say that,' he hissed, as he passed He Who Always Knows Best.

CHAPTER 25

Luis and his men had arrived at the Rio Grande in good time. Their ride had been uneventful. They were reasonably certain that they hadn't been seen, except by the odd shepherd tending his flock high up on the hills. They would never leave their sheep to hurry down into the valley to inform Raoul about the movement of a large number of Luis's men. Anyhow it was none of their business. If there was going to be a battle today they would be well out of it up where they were. Even if Luis won and took over the town again it wouldn't affect them. It would be just a case of one corrupt mayor taking over from another.

'Make sure the men are well hidden.' Luis gave the order to Savales.

Some of the younger men began to climb the trees. The older ones chose vantage points behind the trees, where they would be out of sight of anybody crossing the river.

'That's no good,' said Luis, irritably. 'I want you all up in the trees. Raoul will be arriving here shortly. He'll be coming along this path. You'll never manage to keep the trees between yourselves and Raoul's men. Someone will be bound to see you and then the whole plan will fail.'

'Some of these men aren't fit enough to climb the trees,' stated Savales.

'Do I have to do all your thinking for you?' said Luis, irritably. 'Let the old men look after the horses. They'll have to be tied up a long way away so that there's no possibility of the horses neighing and warning Raoul of our presence.'

Savales went round giving the orders. He was glad that he was walking around or Luis would have seen the anger on his face at the suggestion that he wasn't carrying out his duties properly. He hoped that in the coming battle Luis would be killed. He knew that it was a terrible thought to harbour and that he would have to confess it to the priest when he eventually took confession again. But Luis was getting more and more unbearable. He didn't know whether he would be able to stand it much longer.

On the mountain path Maria and Rosita were making slow progress down towards the valley. They had started off reasonably quickly when they had left the scene of Maria's struggle. In fact they had covered the first mile or so in very quick time. They had an unspoken desire to get away as quickly as they could from the scene of the tragedy, the consequence of which was that Maria's attacker was lying on the rocks below.

After the initial burst of energy they understandably slowed down. Rosita, who was older and far less fit than Maria, dictated the speed of their progress. At first Maria accepted the pace of her companion but gradually she fretted at the slow pace.

'Can't you go any faster?' she exclaimed, irritably.

'It's all right for you. You're younger,' retorted Rosita.

Maria glanced down at the valley below. They still had a long way to go before reaching the lower slopes of the mountain. At the speed they were going it would probably be another couple of hours before they reached the valley floor. Was there any reason for them to hurry? Why didn't they just carry on as they were? It was reasonable to assume that the proposed battle between Luis's followers and Raoul's soldiers would take some time to resolve. So why did she feel the urgent need to press ahead?

Could it have anything to do with a certain American cavalryman? She tried to put the thought aside, but it persisted. She had thought of Paul several times during the past couple of days. The way he had unhesitatingly shot Luis's henchman, who had tried to abduct her outside the church, had convinced her that she would always be safe with him around. Their journey through the desert, when she had eventually passed out through fatigue and lack of water had already convinced her of this. When she recovered consciousness she had found that he was carrying her. How far he had been carrying her she didn't know. But she guessed it had been for some considerable time, since Paul himself was suffering from fatigue. He was staggering. When eventually he collapsed on the sand they had lain in each other's arms. Their lips were too caked to speak, but they looked into each other's eyes. Although she knew they were near death she had somehow felt at peace. Then, of course, the miracle had happened and the Apaches had appeared.

The more she thought of Paul the more she was convinced that somehow he was in danger. The Aztec strain in her ancestry had come to her aid previously in foreseeing tragic events before they had happened. On one particular occasion they had been skating on a lake outside Paris. The ice had appeared to be quite firm and several people had been enjoying the winter activity. Suddenly she had had a terrible premonition. She had seen a vivid mental picture of one of her friends, Nanette, falling through the ice. She searched feverishly for Nanette. She eventually spotted her on the far side of the lake. She raced towards her, shouting her name as she did so. Unfortunately the noise made by some of the skaters as they shouted happily to each other drowned her efforts to get Nanette's attention. Eventually she did succeed in her effort. Nanette even acknowledged her shout with wave of her hand. It was the last gesture her friend made. Because at that moment the ice opened up and Nanette disappeared below the surface. Her body was never recovered.

Now she had the same premonition that Paul was in danger.

'I'm going on ahead,' she informed Rosita.

'Why don't you wait for me?' demanded her companion.

'Because the man I love is in danger,' she cried, as she raced down the path.

CHAPTER 26

Captain Bingley was riding through the desert at the head of his troop of cavalrymen. The wagon with the money inside was bringing up the rear. They had been riding for about an hour. The desert heat hadn't yet begun to hit them, yet Bingley was feeling uncomfortable. His discomfort was due to the nature of the mission he was under-taking.

He didn't like the mission at all. To deliver the gold and notes that were in the trunk would be an assignment which could have some drawbacks, and he always tried to see the disadvantages of any situation before examining its advantages. For example what if the mayor and his soldiers were not at the river in time. What then? Would they have to hang around until they turned up, or would he proceed into San Caldiz? If the latter, then how would the local inhabitants receive them? He was under no illusions that Americans, and for him that meant the Eleventh Cavalry, weren't too popular in San Caldiz. The reason wasn't too far to find. The soldiers had regularly strayed over the border in search of Apaches. In fact the excursions had become so regular that the Mexican farmers had complained to the President of Mexico himself. This had led to the president complaining to a fellow president – the American President, no less. The upshot was that the Eleventh Cavalry had been forcefully reminded that they should not stray over the border, namely the river. Yet here he was, an American, about to assassinate a Mexican who presumably would be sitting on a horse in his own country. The situation didn't bear thinking about. Major wars had been started for less reason than that.

What was Major Linton thinking about? Why had he gone along with Callaghan's crazy scheme? The only reason he could think of was that the major was approaching retiring age. Camp gossip had it that he would be retiring in about six months' time. Well, if he was going to sanction madcap schemes such as this, then the sooner he retired the better.

Of course it was all Callaghan's fault. There was no doubt about it. Nobody but a crazy Irishman would think of such a scheme There were as many holes in it as in a colander. For instance, what if the

Mexicans, seeing that their leader had been shot, started shooting back at them? He only had a dozen men at his disposal – the major having informed him that to have double that number would have made the Mexicans feel nervous. He had pressed for at least half a dozen more men. But the major had been adamant. A dozen men would be quite adequate to carry out the delivery of the money to the Mayor of San Caldiz, he had been positively informed.

Then what about the plan itself: to shoot the mayor – this guy Manuel? Callaghan had said that he would be riding next to him. He would give the signal to shoot the Mexican by putting his hand on his shoulder. What a stupid idea. In the first place it assumed that Callaghan would have pride of place and be riding next to Manuel. In the second place it assumed that the sharpshooters who were accompanying him would be able to shoot Manuel. These three weren't in any special category of sharpshooters. They could probably hit a target at practice on the range five times out of ten. But that wouldn't place them in any special class of expert shot. They might even shoot Callaghan himself by mistake. Bingley permitted himself a smile at the thought.

There was only one person who could be guaranteed to hit a person who was on a horse on the other side of the river and that was Callaghan himself. Although he hated to admit that Callaghan had any outstanding qualities, there was no doubt that as a marksman he was in a class of his own. He had seen him hit the bull's-eye in the target on the rifle range ten times out of ten. Then ask for it to be moved back fifty yards. And then hit it again ten times out of ten.

The more he thought about shooting Manuel the more the possibilities loomed of the whole thing going horribly wrong. If it did he would be the one who would be carrying the can. He would be the fall-guy. He knew that Callaghan had lost his stripes for insubordination. The thought of him, himself, being demoted was too horrible to contemplate. As he rode at the head of his men a worried frown creased his face.

He would have been even more worried if he had known that a war party consisting of a couple of dozen Apaches were trailing them at a safe distance.

CHAPTER 27

Maria found that running down a mountain path was a rapid form of progress, particularly since she didn't have to wait for Rosita. In fact she found the run was exhilarating. If she hadn't dreaded what she was going to find when she arrived at San Caldiz she would have whooped for joy.

As she sped along she tried to concentrate on her vision of the fate that was going to befall her beloved Paul. But the picture stubbornly refused to become any clearer. She could see dozens of soldiers milling about. It suggested that there must be a clash between them and Luis's men.

Would she arrive in time? The one positive shred of knowledge which she gleaned from her vision was that Paul was in terrible danger. She must arrive at the battle in time to warn him.

The bottom of the path was now only a couple of hundred yards ahead. She was thankful that she was fit, due the exercises which she had been forced to do in Paris. Not that she had particularly minded them. In fact she had enjoyed most of them. Now she was reaping the benefits from them as she reached the bottom of the path in record time.

The path came out between San Caldiz and the river. However, she knew that she had about four miles to go before reaching the scene of the battle. She set off along the wide track which would take her there. As she ran she tried to listen for the sounds of rifle fire. So far she had heard none. She knew that the sounds of gunfire carried a considerable distance. But would it carry from the river to her position?

When she had been in Paris she had neglected her visits to church. They had tended to be occasional rather than regular. Now she resolved that if Paul were saved she would go to church every day. She tried to quicken her pace but discovered that the descent down the mountain had taken more from her stamina than she had anticipated. In fact her movements had now become rather disjointed. She would run for a short distance, then she would be forced to walk as she struggled to get her breath.

Another thing that was taking toll of her strength was the fact that now she was running on the plain. The terrain consisted of baked sand interspersed with occasional tufts of coarse grass. It was flat and easy to run on. The one thing that militated against her, however, was the sun. It was draining her energy, just as it had when they had been in the desert. A few times she glanced up at it. But pitilessly it sent its scorching rays to torment her.

As she staggered along her mind began to wander. She imagined that she was back in the desert again with Paul. They were riding on a horse together. She was clinging to him and although they were riding bareback the discomfort was nothing compared to the fact that they were together. It had been a short period of undiluted pleasure. Then the sickening sun had started to claim them. It had been slowly roasting them as surely as any animal on a spit. It had first dried their skin as it was now drying hers. Then it had tormented them because they had had no water. She had no water now.

She shook her head to try to clear her mind. What was she thinking about, dwelling on the time they had spent together in the desert? She had to concentrate on reaching Paul in time to warn him of the danger he was in. She must pull herself together, as her old aunt had often advised her. Was that the sound of gunfire? She stopped in order to try to hear more clearly. Her heavy breathing combined with the pounding of her heart meant that her senses weren't functioning as they should. She listened for a few moments but there was no repeated noise. Maybe it hadn't been gunfire in the first place. Or maybe one of the farmers whom she occasionally passed in their fields had been shooting some birds or animals.

'Come on, no slacking,' she admonished herself in the words of her old games-mistress, and obeying, she staggered forward slowly and painfully.

CHAPTER 28

From their position along the bank of the river, Raoul and his men waited for the arrival of the Eleventh Cavalry with their consignment of money for his bank. Raoul was satisfied with the way things had gone up to now. He had managed to conceal his hatred of his companion, who was now sitting on his horse by his side. In fact he rather prided himself on the way he had managed to deceive Paul. He had been forced to spend over an hour in his company and not once had he hinted at the fact that his hatred was so intense that it could only end up one way – in Paul's death.

While they were waiting for the Americans to appear Raoul had time to contemplate exactly how he would kill Paul. Of course, he would like Paul's death to be slow and painful. He had several instruments of torture in the prison in the castle – some of which had even been inherited from the

Spaniards, from when they were indulging in their own pastime of torturing – in the name of the Inquisition. Some of these implements were still in remarkably good condition. They had been kept in working order by the presidents who had successively ruled Mexico. And who had been happy to carry on the old tradition of torture.

Regretfully, Raoul had to dismiss that extremely pleasant idea. He had to consider that he was now an upright citizen. As such he would shortly be accepting American money for his bank. Callaghan was an American citizen. If it ever leaked out that he had been thrown in prison and tortured by the bank owner, then Mr Greer would undoubtedly want his money back in quick time. So, regretfully, he would have to think again about which method of disposing of his companion.

He glanced at him as though trying to divine whether Paul had any inkling of his thoughts. But Paul was staring straight ahead, hoping to spot the arrival of the Eleventh Cavalry.

Paul knew that the cavalry should be arriving shortly. If they had started on time, as he would have expected, then Raoul shouldn't have to wait too long for his money to arrive. In fact, Raoul's life would be coming to an end on the arrival of his money. Paul knew that he should feel some remorse at being the means of bringing a fellow member of the human race to his death. But, instead, his main feeling was one of expectancy. In his opinion the man sitting on the horse next to him was one of the vilest of humans and he would have no compunctions in killing him himself. But the way he had chosen to get rid of Raoul should ensure that he would get away with the assassination.

At that moment Paul saw the tell-tale sign of a cloud of dust in the desert. It meant that Bingley and his cavalrymen were on their way. He guessed that they were still about a couple of miles away, but they should arrive in about ten minutes' time.

'The Cavalry are on their way,' he informed Raoul.

The information soon filtered along the ranks. Raoul's soldiers were spaced out along the river and they greeted the news with eager anticipation that their enforced waiting would soon be over. Luis's men, who were hidden in the trees behind the soldiers, also sensed that something would soon be happening. They gripped their rifles tighter and concentrated their aim on the nearest soldier.

'It won't be long now,' said Raoul.

Paul wondered why he felt that there was some hidden meaning in those apparently harmless words. Could Raoul possibly have foreseen that he had arranged for his assassination? No, there was no possible way that he could have foreseen that.

Everything was going according to his plan. He couldn't see any possible way that things would go wrong.

But the next minute he was forced to revise his opinion. Things were starting to go wrong already. Raoul, instead of staying by his side, had began to ride his horse slowly along the ranks of soldiers. He was talking to them, telling them that he wanted them to keep still. He explained that the Americans who would be arriving shortly were trained cavalrymen. They would sit on their horses for ages while the animals stayed still. He wanted to impress the Americans that they could also do the same thing.

Paul fumed as he watched Raoul proceeding slowly along the line. Raoul was taking a devilishly long time in talking to his soldiers. As the minutes ticked by the cavalry were drawing ever nearer. What if they arrived at the far bank and Raoul wasn't by his side? How could he point out to Bingley that this was the man to be killed?

Paul watched Raoul's irritatingly slow progress with growing desperation.

CHAPTER 29

The Indians who had been following the wagon had been doing so at a discreet distance. They had been able to keep at least a couple of miles back from the cavalrymen since it was easy to follow the trail in the sand. Also they could depend on the keen sight of Eyes Like a Hawk to inform them if the cavalrymen stopped suddenly in order to assuage their thirst.

They had managed to keep roughly the same distance between them and the wagon for almost the whole of the journey through the desert, but as they neared the end of their journey some of the younger braves became over-anxious. They began to move forward more quickly than the older ones, who had followed the advice of Lion in the Hills of keeping back, out of sight of the cavalrymen. The young braves were given a stern warning on a couple of occasions by their self-appointed chief, but with the scent of the river coming nearer they ignored him and rode ahead more quickly than before. The result was twofold. In the first place, Lion in the Hills was forced to ride ahead quickly to catch up with them. In the second place, he lost his temper and berated them for their thoughtlessness. He called them every kind of vermin he could lay his tongue to.

But the damage had been done. A young cavalryman who had dropped behind the others because his horse had picked up a foreign object in his shoe, suddenly looked up from removing the piece of grit. He almost fainted when he saw a war party of Apaches not a few hundred yards away.

'Apaches! Apaches!' he yelled as he jumped on his horse more quickly than he had ever done in his life, and raced to rejoin the others.

His shouts were at first greeted with disbelief, which quickly changed to horror as the full import of his warning hit the small band of cavalrymen. A quick count told Bingley that there were twice as many Apaches as cavalrymen. The fact that they had donned their war paint meant that their presence was no coincidence. It didn't take a genius to deduce that they were after the chest with the money in it. He wasn't used to giving orders on the spur of the moment, but this order he gave without hardly giving it a thought.

'Get to the river,' he shouted. 'Move!'

He nursed a vague hope that if they could get to the river the Mexican soldiers on the other side would come to his aid. The cavalrymen needed no further bidding. They had all glimpsed the frightening sight of the Apaches in full war paint. Many of them were too young to have seen such a sight before. Whatever were their mixed reactions the uppermost thought in everybody's mind was to reach the safety of the river before they were attacked by the black demons behind them.

The Apaches rapidly closed the distance between them and the Eleventh Cavalry. The soldiers were hampered in their progress by the presence of the wagon, which had once taken pride of place on their travels but was now an undoubted hindrance.

The cavalrymen were getting nearer to the river, but at the same time the Indians were getting closer to them. The race was decided when one of the Apaches, who was slightly in front of the others, fired an arrow which hit one of the two horses which had been pulling the wagon. The horse immediately stumbled, pulling its companion down with it.

Again Bingley acted out of character. Without thinking he quickly shot the distressed horse and ordered the cavalrymen to untie the other horse. By now the cavalrymen had reached a position near enough to the river for those on the opposite bank to see exactly what was going on. Paul was the first to react. The sight of his comrades being attacked by a war party of Apaches drove all thought of his preconceived plan from his head. He instinctively spurred his horse and rode into the river.

Raoul was at first taken aback by Paul's reaction. Then, realizing that the person he had vowed to kill was on the point of disappearing he fired a couple of shots at him. One of them was near enough to pluck Paul's sleeve. He turned in his saddle to see who was shooting at him from behind. He identified Raoul as his would-be assassin. A further shot from Raoul's rifle, which just passed over his head, confirmed Paul's impression.

In normal circumstances Paul would have stopped and exchanged shots with Raoul, but the situation in front of him demanded that he gave it priority. Raoul would have to wait and he would deal with him later. Paul rode the short distance to join his comrades. Already arrows were being aimed at them as they crouched around the wagon. Paul rode up and jumped off his horse, taking up his position on the wagon alongside Bingley.

'Welcome aboard,' said Bingley.

The rest of the cavalrymen were busy trying to get shots at the Indians who were circling the wagon at high speed on their horses.

'Shoot their horses,' yelled Paul.

There was a pause in the firing. For a cavalry-man to shoot a horse was almost on a par with desecrating a holy relic in a church. A horse was a sacred animal which the cavalryman had been taught to look after before he tended to his own creature comforts.

'They stole the horses in the first place,' Paul explained. 'We can do what we like with them.'

So saying he brought one of the horses down with a shot. The Indian was forced to jump off it as it fell. This gave Paul an easy target which he picked off with his rifle.

While this battle was raging another had started up less than a quarter of a mile away. Raoul's soldiers, seeing their chief firing at Paul, had assumed that their battle was starting. The fact that they were bored with their inactivity also probably had something to do with their next move. They started to follow Paul into the river. They assumed that they were going to fight the Apaches and that Raoul's shots had been a warning to the Indians who were attacking the cavalrymen.

This forward movement of Raoul's men produced an unexpected reaction.

Luis, perched up in the trees, saw that his intended enemy was about to disappear. Realizing that he had come all that way and was in danger of not having a battle at the end of it, he followed the only course open to him.

'Fire!' he shouted.

The first volley from his outlaws killed or wounded half a dozen of Raoul's soldiers. Their immediate reaction was to turn and try to find out who was attacking them from behind. The source of the bullets was easy to identify since Luis's men had brushed away the leaves which had been hiding them in order to have a clear sight of the soldiers who were now in the middle of the river.

'It's Luis and his men,' shouted Raoul, unnecessarily. His advice which followed: 'Kill them,' was eagerly seized upon by his soldiers.

The two battles were raging independently. The one was as fierce as the other with no quarter asked and none given. The battle in the desert was particularly bloodthirsty. The sight of one of the cavalrymen who had been killed by the Apaches, then being lassoed until they could drag his body away from the vicinity of the conflict was the catalyst which turned the affair into one of the bloodiest for years. The Indian then calmly proceeded to scalp the soldier. While some of the cavalry were being visibly sick, Paul shot the Indian in the head.

The scalping had an unexpected effect on the cavalry. Whereas until then not all of them had followed Paul's advice to shoot the horses, particularly the older men who had formed a strong bond between themselves and their horses, now they obeyed Paul's instruction without hesitation. They eagerly searched for any Indian who was still circling the cavalrymen and tried to see that at least he wouldn't be in a position to scalp one of them.

The one who was having most success with killing the Apaches was Paul. He had taken up a kneeling position using the side of the wagon as a shelter. He was so efficient at picking off the Indians that Lion in the Hills, having lost almost half of his warriors, contemplated calling a halt to the killing. But a few of his young braves had other ideas. They had abandoned their horses, having seen the accuracy of some of the cavalrymen's bullets. Instead they began a manoeuvre which had worked in favour of the Indians for centuries. They prepared a couple of fire arrows. These they lit and shot into the middle of the wagon. The canvas caught fire in no time. Soon the wagon was blazing merrily.

'Get away from the wagon,' shouted Paul.

The cavalrymen didn't need to be given any further instructions; they followed Paul without hesitation. Luckily the smoke from the fire had partly covered their movement and they were able to gather at a safe distance from the burning wagon with only two casualties. Once there they formed a square on Paul's instructions.

The expected Indian attack however didn't materialize. The Apaches were more intent on trying to put out the fire that they had started than following the cavalrymen. Paul summed up the situation.

'Right. Run as you've never run before,' he shouted, following his own advice and now racing towards the river.

A few desultory shots were aimed after them, but if any of the cavalrymen had broken their flight to look behind them they would have seen that the Indians were now throwing sand on the wagon as they attempted to put out the blaze.

The cavalrymen reached the river. At about the same time the Indians had managed to put out the fire. The pulled the charred chest away from the wagon by the expedient of using their lasso ropes. Once away from the wagon they set about opening the chest. This proved more difficult than they had imagined since it was still extremely hot. However, in the end they succeeded. When the chest was opened they delved into it eagerly. Their expressions changed to surprise and then to anger.

'Where are the guns you promised us?' demanded one bitterly disappointed young brave.

Lion in the Hills was the first one to recover from the huge disappointment.

'If you take some of the money you will be able to buy all the guns you want,' he countered.

A disappointed war party stuffed their saddle-bags with the dollars, which were in neat bundles in the chest.

'What about the gold?' queried their chief. 'Don't any of you want the gold?'

'How are we going to carry it?' demanded one of the braves, whose bag was already full with the twenty-dollar notes.

One of the braves seized a handful of gold coins and tossed them into the air. They came down in a shower and lay half-buried in the sand. Other braves followed suit. Soon they were all gathering gold coins, flinging them into the air and shouting with glee as they descended on to the sand. Paul and the rest of the cavalry, who were watching them from the river, stared in amazement at their antics. One of the older cavalrymen summed it up.

'One minute they are behaving like savages and the next you would think they are schoolchildren,' he announced.

'That's it then,' said Bingley, with massive relief. 'It's all over.'

'It might be for you,' said Paul, turning his attention to the battle which was still raging on the other bank of the river. 'I've still got some unfinished business.'

It was obvious that the struggle between Raoul's soldiers and Luis's outlaws had been a bitter and bloody one, judging by the corpses who were now lying around, some of them were on the bank, but some were in the river, where they were floating slowly towards the sea. The two forces had given up the use of guns and were now engaged in close-quarter fighting. It seemed to Paul that Raoul's soldiers were holding the upper hand since they were using bayonets while the outlaws were depending on swords.

Paul eagerly scanned the mêlée for signs of Raoul. In fact it was Raoul who found Paul, or rather his bullet did, since it passed uncomfortably close to his ear. Paul instinctively dived into the river. Although Raoul aimed another few bullets in his direction they were more in hope than in expectation that they would hit Paul.

In the brief moment before he dived into the river Paul had spotted exactly where Raoul was hiding. It was behind some trees slightly away from the fighting. When Paul came out from the river he had purposely emerged a few hundred yards downstream in order not to give Raoul a clear shot at him again.

Paul proceeded to advance cautiously towards Raoul, using the trees as cover. The only disadvantage from Paul's point of view was that he now didn't have a weapon, his rifle having been rendered useless when he dived into the river. As he passed some of the corpses of the outlaws who had obviously been shot when they were emerging from the trees he glanced at them, searching for a weapon he could use. There were several rifles lying about, but these were old models and he didn't know whether there was any suitable ammunition for them. Also he realized that time was running out. Raoul was not going to wait indefinitely for him to turn up.

He eventually chose the only weapon he could find – a sword. It was a double-bladed sword – the kind he had used when he had been an officer and had had instructions under an extremely enthusiastic sergeant.

He found Raoul sitting behind a tree, staring intently at the river.

'Here I am,' Paul announced.

Raoul swung round. His face was wreathed in hatred as he took a shot at his arch enemy.

Paul had anticipated the shot and dived behind a tree just in time. Raoul attempted to get another shot at him but the *click* from his rifle informed him that he had ran out of ammunition. Still, he had his rifle and the bayonet in it was definitely more effective than the sword Paul was now wielding. Raoul stepped into the open space, his lips set in a snarl of anticipation as he prepared to end Paul's life.

Paul realized that if the conflict went on for any length of time the superior weight of Raoul's rifle would overcome his sword's comparatively light weight. As they circled each other a trick which the sergeant had played on him at their practice occurred to him. He knew that if it didn't succeed then the chances of his surviving the present duel would be extremely slim. He did what the sergeant had shown him those months ago – he dropped on one knee.

The move took Raoul by surprise. Raoul's reaction was to hesitate. It was a fatal mistake; Paul had a perfect target. He drove his sword upwards into Raoul's heart. Raoul died instantly.

'That was a risky thing to do.' Maria had appeared by his side.

'Since when have you become an expert on using a sword?'

'I used to use one when I was in Paris. My instructor always said that that manoeuvre was a risky thing to do.'

They were standing close to each other and Paul knew that he was grinning like a schoolboy. What the hell? Maria was here, that was the important thing.

Bingley came up to them.

'Luis has been killed,' he stated. 'I think we can safely say it's all over.'

'We haven't started yet,' said Paul, as he took Maria in his arms and kissed her.